The Equinox
NIGHTMARE

Thank you for coming to my event. Hope you enjoy the "Nightmares." Feel free to register your opinion on Amazon - helps with the marketing.

Sincerely, Mark
Nov. 4, 2019

MARK MARONDE

Copyright © 2016 Mark Maronde
All rights reserved
First Edition

PAGE PUBLISHING, INC.
New York, NY

First originally published by Page Publishing, Inc. 2016

ISBN 978-1-68289-408-8 (pbk)
ISBN 978-1-68289-409-5 (digital)

Printed in the United States of America

THE LONELY PATH TO FREEDOM

Sasha practiced her piano lesson, while Marc stared emotionlessly out the family room window. The rain hadn't ceased in the past twenty-four hours, only slowed to a steady drizzle once.

What kind of woman could just abandon her daughter? he wondered as he finished a glass of iced water. He got it, that she didn't care much for the life as an ambassador's wife. Ginny had been a human resources director at a major U.S. hospital. Her son, Mikey, had proven to be a handful, as many teenagers are. She'd never accepted the fact that Mikey enjoyed the company of the young ladies, and even several attractive, lonely wives!

Complaints placed at the embassy did manage to reach the beleaguered president. With so much turmoil in the region and an upcoming election, he ordered the embassy staff to return to Washington immediately. Marc remembered all too well the sick, empty feeling when he returned to the embassy with Sasha from her final piano lesson. His personal assistant, Adrienne, ushered Sasha into her room to pack, while the embassy security hustled about, making certain all areas were secured. A young marine gestured to the limo driver; Marc joined them, hoping that they were out of Sasha's hearing.

Gunfire erupted in the distance, followed by an explosion that rattled the building's contents. The young marine warned, "You haven't much time to get to safety! You'll be leaving through the rear of the embassy. One marine will ride shotgun to provide security. Your wife and stepson left on the final commercial flight earlier this afternoon." Marc's jaw dropped; he absorbed all this information. The protesters reached the embassy's front gates, shouting anti-American slogans. Marc grabbed his laptop, accessories, and hoisted Sasha to his shoulder with his free hand. Adrienne grabbed Sasha's overnight bag and started out the back. Once all were safely in the limo, Marc looked back once to view marines exchange gunfire with rebels in an effort to defend the U.S. embassy.

He shook his head slightly and placed his empty glass on an end table. Sasha continued playing piano. She had not spoken of her mother since that chaotic day. Adrienne stayed on as his assistant and truly enjoyed being a surrogate mother of sorts to Sasha. Life progressed favorably. It was as though he had never been an ambassador.

Sasha finished her lesson and quietly walked to the kitchen for a snack. Adrienne had taken the night off. Marc retrieved his empty glass, followed her to the kitchen, and prepared a snack for himself. They sat together at the kitchen table and ate in silence. Marc pondered the future.

THE GAMBLER

In the mobile home community, everyone blended together well. No one would expect their neighbors to be a part of the witness protection program. The most attractive family consisted of a thirtyish brunette, her geeky pencil-pushing husband, a boy (twenty), a girl (nineteen), and a rather rotund brother-in-law. The geeky husband and his obese brother once skimmed profits from mob-owned casinos and, worse yet, ratted them out to federal authorities in regard to money laundering. The casino boss, Antonio, was extremely pissed off. He offered a large cash reward to anyone who reported to him the snitches' whereabouts.

It didn't take long for Sasha to make new friends at school. Adrienne relished her role as nanny / housekeeper / Marc's personal assistant. The only hiccup in this arrangement occurred the day a courier arrived with divorce papers for Marc to sign. He stared at the paperwork; the courier twirled a pen patiently. It was a wonderfully sunny summer morning. Marc signed the papers, accepted his copies, and closed the door abruptly. Sasha stood by Adrienne; both remained silent.

Adrienne broke the silence. "We have a busy day planned, Marc!" she announced "Our music program at school is in dire need of funding, so our summer class is helping by collecting aluminum cans that the litterbugs throw in our streets!"

Marc nodded responsively. "I have two final exams to give this morning, one in U.S. history since 1945 and the other in twenty-first century terrorism. Definitely a lot less stressful to teach it than to live it." Adrienne frowned at him, gesturing to Sasha. Marc shook his head.

"Hey, baby girl, why don't the three of us grill out by the pool tonight?"

Sasha looked up at Adrienne, who nodded approvingly.

Summer school was nothing like he had remembered all those years ago. He parked his 1971 Firebird in the faculty section and started across the quad. He encountered three football players bullying a slender-built teen boy. "Faggot! Faggot!" they all chanted in sync. "Go back to San Fran, Fairy Boy!" And then the leader (Marc assumed) dumped the teen's books.

"OK, playtime's over, guys," Marc informed them. "Knock off this shit and get to class, *now*! This damn bullying can get you all suspended, not to mention your asses charged with hate crimes!"

The leader of the bullies stood in Marc's path and snarled, "We don't have classes. We're studying video with Coach! You're just a substitute teacher here. Our parents can get you fired!"

Marc just laughed and then, in a low, menacing tone, stated, "You three fucking jocks have no clue who I am or where I came from. But not one more word out of any of you. I *will* rain holy hell down on all of you!"

Two of the bullies pulled their leader back. "It's not worth it, Jay! He's a fucking psycho! He might be one of them—you never know!"

He watched to be certain that the three athletes actually were going to the gym. Satisfied that they were, he turned to the teen, who'd since picked up his books. "Does this shit occur on a daily basis?" he asked. The student nodded, ashamed. "Hold your head high, kid!" Marc demanded. "People need to learn to respect the differences in each other! I think it's time they learned that valuable lesson, sooner rather than later!" The teen thanked him and hurried off to class.

Final exams for the summer term passed without incident. Needing to stretch his legs, Marc moved from behind his desk and walked to the window. Gazing emotionlessly, he was somewhat surprised to see a large number of people strolling along the highway. No one collected any aluminum cans; the walkers shuffled without purpose. Frowning, Marc returned to his desk and shuffled papers till the bell rang.

The drive home seemed eerily somber. The presence of the walkers heightened a sense of foreboding. Marc noted that all the walkers appeared to be only high school and college aged. He continued toward town, where the streets were desolate. The shops, all dark, added to Marc's sense of disaster on the horizon. He tried to reach Adrienne on his cell phone.

Sasha splashed around her kiddie pool then raced to her daddy as he joined Adrienne on the patio. Marc wanted to question Adrienne about the day's events but decided against it when Sasha bounded merrily onto his lap. "We picked up all the cans!" she exclaimed. Adrienne patted her shoulder, and Sasha continued, "Now our class has money for new band instruments!" Marc smiled and rocked his daughter gently. "Are you feeling all right, Daddy?" she asked as Adrienne started the grill. All seemed well, but Marc simply couldn't shake the uneasiness he'd felt since midafternoon.

The city's west end had been in a state of steady decline since the 1990s, and as a result, there was no resistance when the foreign invaders took charge and ended the residents' communication with the rest of the city. Senior citizens who could not afford to move years earlier felt that Russians had finally made good on their Cold War–era promises.

No one was permitted to enter or exit Sector 9, as the west end was now known as, without permission from the commandant. Dylan, the news director and owner of the city's only radio station, protested this action vehemently. The commandant, enraged, ordered his officers to arrest Dylan and take over his radio station.

Even with the newly imposed martial law, residents in Sector 9 still hosted barbecues, bag tosses, and any other activity that encouraged consumption of alcoholic beverages. Several high-ranking officers of the commandant lingered outside a pub, talking openly of Dylan's imminent arrest. Within minutes, Dylan had been tipped off by one of his listeners, a former employee of the city's public works department. The employee assisted Dylan in escape through the sewer system to freedom. Once in the city's central business district, Dylan emerged from the stench of the sewer near a friend's shop, fortunately. His benefactor, however, was summarily executed upon his return to Sector 9. The commandant then ordered the execution of the man's family.

Outraged, Dylan and his friends formed a resistance of sorts, with their primary goal being to inform everyone of the recent invasion/takeover of the city's west end. Dylan began broadcasting from the college's radio station. Sadly, not many residents took Dylan's frightening news reports of Sector 9 and its atrocities seriously. Angrily Dylan invited the city's residents to drive to the west end and view the changes: the offices, no entrance or exit, guard towers, the fence, and such.

With the summer term having ended at the college, Dylan persisted in transmitting his message regarding the unknown invaders. The dean of students remembered Dylan as a graduate student and offered him the use of the college's radio station. The college board recommended Dylan be hired as a political science instructor.

The city's residents consciously opted to remain willfully ignorant of the west end residents' enslavement, despite Dylan's warnings. This truly distressed him, but he continued to warn people daily on his radio show. He hoped to reach more listeners before the fall term began; he was unsure of how many would tune in to an evening show.

Adrienne, Sasha, and Marc ate in silence. Adrienne suspected that Marc was preoccupied and questioned him regarding his day. Marc shook his head, rubbed his eyes, and answered, "I'm fine, just one of those days. A strange day, at that. A lot of young people, many of them college students, walked aimlessly along the main highway this afternoon. They all stared rather listlessly. It was very unusual."

Sasha passed a handbill to her dad and chimed, "I found this when we were collecting cans!"

Marc accepted it and read aloud, "We are no longer free. The city's west end has been seized by foreign invaders! The mayor refuses to acknowledge this has occurred, so now we must fight for our own freedom! Listen to my radio show daily on…" Marc's voice trailed off. Adrienne and Sasha stared inquisitively. "Dylan wouldn't make up such a story," he resumed speaking. "No way. He's been hired to teach government, and I believe he is department head for political science."

Adrienne began to clear the table. "Did anything unusual happen today?" she inquired.

Marc concentrated deeply for a few moments and responded, "No, not really. A bullying incident before exams. No, the kids were strangely quiet, even for finals. The walkers were silent too."

Sasha laughed. Adrienne raised her eyebrows incredulously. Marc explained the throng of coeds walking along the main highway. Adrienne checked Marc's temperature. "No fever," she stated.

Marc raised his hand and dismissed her with a wave. "I am *not* making this up! Something strange is happening, and I will check it out in the morning when I go post the grades." Sasha continued to laugh as Adrienne prodded her toward the kitchen. He rubbed his eyes, finished his iced tea, and gazed fixedly at the night sky. A full moon rose in the starry night. Marc relaxed and read the newspaper.

The next morning, Adrienne and Sasha prepared breakfast. Marc slept in. Adrienne advised Sasha to be quiet. "Your daddy's been working hard. He needs some rest. We're going downtown to shop. I'll clean up this kitchen later." Happily Sasha finished her cereal.

Moments later, they made their way through the customary number of patrons downtown. In the distance, Adrienne thought she heard a steady humming of Petula Clark's classic, "Downtown," and found it rather unnerving. Sasha paid it no mind and gazed into the various store windows.

The casino boss, Antonio, did not give a rat's behind about the slow, subtle social changes in the city, as well as the menacing political undercurrent. He wanted his money; patience had never been his strongest trait. Staring out his office window in Las Vegas, he read a text message from his number 1 collection agent, Santino. A sly smile engulfed his usual agitated demeanor, and he responded with an explicit directive to eliminate the entire family upon collecting the debt. No witness protection program could save anyone from his wrath, especially when the snitches stupidly elected to openly gamble in one of his east casinos! Santino enjoyed his job, Antonio mused. That thing he had for setting fires.

Santino sat patiently in his classic black 1967 Lincoln at the mobile home community's entrance, sipping a Starbuck's coffee. Residents paid him no mind as they passed him on the way out to begin the day. He listened emotionlessly to the heated argument in a nearby double-wide. The wife, hysterical, screamed, "All this cash! Are you insane? You may have blown our cover!"

Santino grinned and started the Lincoln.

The quarrel abruptly ceased when Santino pounded on the trailer's front door. Trudy, the wife, grabbed her children, Sam and Jackie, and raged, "You bastards! All you cared about was winning more money!" She stared at her brother-in-law and continued, "Fat Eddie, you selfish pig! You brought the mob into our lives!" Santino chuckled softly as he kept pounding on the door. Then he began pouring gasoline around the trailer. Trudy maneuvered her children toward a crawl space. Santino returned to the front door and opened it with a pry bar. Trudy and the children escaped through the crawl space. Fat Eddie attempted to follow, but Santino ordered him, at gunpoint, to return to the living room. He motioned Trudy's husband, Tom, to place all the cash in a duffel bag. Trudy and the children gasped at the stench of the gasoline and ran to a nearby cornfield.

Santino glanced out the kitchen window as the three escaped safely into the cornfield and laughed heartily. "This is your lucky day, gents! I don't kill women and kids! Especially those who have suffered because of two pathetic losers such as yourselves!" Tom finished securing the cash and pushed the duffel bag to Santino. Santino accepted it and, in an exchange of sorts, dropped a Mason jar of gasoline onto the table. Tom sat quietly, paling as he urinated in his pants. The gasoline trickled across the table. Fat Eddie waddled to the crawl space. Santino shot both men in their knees and calmly strolled out the door. Once outside, he made a Molotov cocktail, lit it, and tossed it through an open window. As he drove away, he relished hearing the screams of Tom and Fat Eddie. Patting the duffel bag on the Lincoln's front seat, he swerved to avoid hitting a black cat.

Trudy, Sam, and Jackie never looked back; all three trembled slightly as they heard the gunshots, the men's horrific cries for mercy. The stench of the burning trailer motivated them to run faster through the germinating stalks of corn. "Hopefully Farmer Ron won't be pissed," Sam offered. Trudy gazed back at him. "He speaks to the FFA classes—he is very particular about his field's appearance!"

Marc posted the grades for both classes' final exams. As he cleaned out his desk, Dylan stopped by. "So this is it then," he stated. "What's next for the former diplomat?"

Marc chuckled and responded, "Didn't think anyone knew that. By the way, congratulations on your new position here at the college! Yeah, I'll probably just sub for a while after I get my daughter ready for elementary school this fall." He finished in the classroom and started to leave. Quietly he added, "Keep up with what you're doing on radio, Dylan. I drove to the west end. This Sector 9 crap is *not* to my liking. I have a feeling that our city is headed in a dark, disturbing direction!" Dylan nodded solemnly.

Trudy, Sam, and Jackie ran for what seemed like hours through the cornfield. The horrific screams and the stench of the men burning in the trailer remained indelibly imprinted on them. Finally, the three reached the end of the field and tumbled into the backyard, exhausted, to find a young girl playing alone with her dolls. She sang, softly but audibly, Petula Clark's classic song, "Downtown." She paid no attention to the three strangers and poured tea for her dolls.

Dylan and Marc finished their conversation. Marc gathered his belongings from his desk, secured them in the trunk of his car, and started for home. As he passed by the downtown, he noticed an unusually large police presence. What few shoppers there were moved slowly and methodically, like programmed robots. Marc slowed to observe; he turned to listen as a woman's screams echoed inside a police van. Dylan wasn't kidding, he realized, about the ever-increasing police state. Preoccupied with other thoughts, he continued on, and upon arriving home, bolted from the car to discover three strangers talking to Sasha. *Where the hell is Adrienne?* he wondered. Santino smirked arrogantly as he passed the point at which Marc maneuvered into his driveway. *My Lincoln is more classy than that Firebird,* he huffed as he continued on to the city limits. Happy to be finished with his current mission, he turned on the radio, lit a Cuban cigar, and settled back for the long drive back to Vegas. A news broadcast interrupted his favorite classic rock music; the announcer's voice crackled, "We are under an order of martial law, signed by executive order of the president earlier today. A curfew of sunset shall be enforced…"

Santino angrily threw his cigar out the window and called Antonio. No reception. He sent a text message and continued on. A convey of military police vehicles passed; the occupants attired in riot gear eyed him suspiciously. Sweating profusely, Santino veered onto the parking lot of a convenience store to read a text message from Antonio. His neck muscles tensed as he read the message, "Get out of that city, NOW! Martial law declared in many towns across U.S.—only text message, tower monitored." Approximately twenty-five soldiers surrounded Santino. The sun slowly set. A soft twilight breeze created a chill. "Get the hell away from my daughter, *now*!" Marc thundered.

Sam responded, "We need help! Hey, I know you from school!"

Jackie added, "Yeah, I was in one of your government classes you subbed in."

Trudy quickly explained their day's events. Marc slumped in a lawn chair to listen. After she finished relating their situation, Marc replied, "Well, you don't want to be out on the streets after dark. Something is going on, I'm not sure exactly what. Soldiers acting like police all over the downtown. I passed a convoy on my way home. My housekeeper and Sasha's nanny, Adrienne, is missing. Well, we can sort it out in the morning. I'll scrounge us up something to eat. You can find something of mine that fits you, Sam. Adrienne has a lot that should fit you ladies."

Sasha stopped humming and remained silent throughout the meal. She ate slowly, deliberately. Sam commented, "You sure don't dress like a typical college instructor in your age group!" Trudy nudged him, but Marc laughed it off. "No, Sam, I sure don't. Had enough wearing suits while a diplomat!" Sam chuckled. Marc's tone grew serious. "We need to have a plan," he began. "I've secured this house as best I can. Keep the living room light off, peep through the curtains. You will notice soldiers patrolling on foot and in vehicles. A young man is slumped against the fence, which surrounds a well-lit power plant." Upon finishing their meal, all checked out Marc's assertions.

Sam waited till Jackie peered through the curtains. She returned to her mother's side. Sasha began to nod off at the dining room table. Marc glanced approvingly as the women helped Sasha get ready for bed. Sam parted the curtains and viewed the scene angrily. *Just what has happened in our city,* he wondered, *to bring about this martial law nonsense?* Marc shook his head sadly, unable to formulate a quick answer. Realizing that it was nearly time for Dylan's evening radio show, he silently reached for the remote to turn it on. Tonight, Dylan's tone was grave, almost somber. "Martial law has been declared," he stated tersely. "Citizens of our city must be off the streets by sunset! Storm troopers patrol our streets. Those who dare speak out *disappear!*" The two men remained speechless throughout Dylan's horrific broadcast. Upon its conclusion, Marc changed to another local station.

"Dylan is extremely brave," Marc declared, "to do such a show from the college."

Both were stunned to listen to a live remote; the station manager's arrest and subsequent removal shocked the city's freedom-loving citizens! Sam stated, "We have to do something."

Marc agreed. "Yes, but first we must formulate a plan to save that young man from the clutches of those fucking Nazi bastards!" Trudy and Jackie joined them, wearing expressions of extreme trepidation.

"Before you guys do anything reckless or dangerous," Trudy interjected, "something isn't quite right with Sasha! She was humming then singing an old song, 'Downtown.' She's asleep now."

Marc nodded and replied, "I know. She's been acting strangely since her nanny disappeared. I just wonder if she may have witnessed whatever happened to Adrienne. She'd been with us for a long time." Sam and Jackie parted the curtain for another look.

"We need a diversion," Sam called out, "one that will distract those soldiers, give us some time to get to that guy!"

Jackie offered, "Well, if Adrienne has some perfume, I can take it, sneak up the street, throw it, and break it open on the pavement. That'll attract them!"

Trudy adamantly opposed to the idea, protesting, "No! It's too dangerous!"

Sam chided, "Come on, Ma, we're college kids now! We can handle it!"

Marc agreed with Sam. "Trudy, we can't just leave that kid, whoever he is, to suffer at the hands of those soldiers!"

She nodded her head resignedly and went back upstairs to check on Sasha.

Jackie showed them one of Adrienne's handbags, filled with various perfumes. "Keep one with a sprayer for yourself," Marc advised. "In case one of the assholes grabs you, you can defend yourself."

Jackie replied, "Oh, if that happens, I'll also kick him in his nuts!" Sam appeared stunned to hear his sister speak so graphically. The three slipped out the back door quietly. Jackie held the handbag tightly so as not to make noise and ran through neighboring backyards. Marc and Sam eased carefully to the front of the house, monitoring the soldiers' actions. Two soldiers stood quietly under the streetlight, chatting in a Russian dialect.

The soldiers' heads turned abruptly at the sounds of broken perfume glass. For extra measure, Jackie hurled one that set off a car alarm. A gentle breeze carried the scent of perfume. Sam started out of the shadows, but Marc restrained him.

"Wait!" he admonished. "There may be a few more soldiers!" Three more emerged from between abandoned homes nearest the water tower. "I saw this when I was still with the embassy. It's an old Soviet tactic to lure insurgents or, in reality, freedom fighters out into the open." After waiting approximately another minute, they raced across the street to the fallen citizen languishing against the fence.

Sam reached him first. "Oh my god!" he exclaimed. "It's my friend Steve! Jackie's boyfriend too!"

Marc stated, "Not so loud! Grab a side of him, and let's get him back to the house. He seems dehydrated." By the time the three reached the house, Steve experienced a bout of dry heaves. The soldiers also noticed what had occurred. They ran back to the water tower, jabbering in their native tongue. Jackie met them at the back fence gate and assisted them in getting Steve inside. "Lock that gate," he directed Jackie. "We have company. Nice job diverting those soldiers' attention!"

She nodded anxiously. "We only saw four, but who knows how many will be out and about after this little mission?"

Once inside, Jackie and Trudy stifled emotional responses to Steve's condition.

Sam handed Marc the first aid kit. Steve had only a few minor scrapes, fortunately. Marc offered him bottled water, and he drank heartily. "I know you're thirsty, kid," Marc began calmly, "but just drink the next one slowly. You don't want those dry heaves again!" Steve accepted a second bottle and sipped it thoughtfully. He struggled to sit up.

"Take it easy, man," Sam advised. Jackie held her boyfriend's hand.

Steve related, "I'd just left baseball practice—summer league finals play-offs start next week. Dylan was broadcasting his usual show, the stuff about Sector 9, martial law, and so on. I didn't even get off the college lot when soldiers blocked my way, dragged me from my car, and beat the crap out of me. I came around, found myself at the fence surrounding the city's water tower. Then, you and Sam..." his voice trailed off. Trudy prepared soup and a sandwich, which he consumed ravenously.

"The bastards are trying to send all freedom lovers a fucking message!" Marc seethed. Trudy bristled at his coarse language. Sam looked at him inquisitively. He continued, "Dylan has tried to warn everyone, but no one listened! I was too involved in adapting to life after the embassy, getting Sasha ready for school this fall, and trying to focus on teaching again. It doesn't look good. We need to contact Dylan!"

An intercom buzzing interrupted Marc's rant. He strolled to the front door and pressed a button to respond.

"We want to inspect your property!" barked the soldier.

Marc sneered, "Blow it out your asses! If you fuck up my locked gates in any way, I will scatter your brains like fucking cherry tomatoes all over the street! Now, go back to your post before I forget that I am the ambassador to your country!"

Sam peered through the curtains. "They've backed away, and they're talking amongst themselves." Marc sighed, and Sam added, "Now all four are walking over to the water tower. You bluffed them!"

Marc didn't share Sam's confidence. "No, it's only a matter of time before they decide to investigate us further," he replied.

Steve slept soundly. The women slept upstairs in Adrienne's room and periodically checked on Sasha. Sam took the first watch, while Marc napped in his favorite recliner. "We need to get some supplies, food and drink, tomorrow," he commented.

Sam responded, "Yeah, we'll probably have a few more soldiers to contend with as well."

Sleep would not come easily for Marc, even in the wee hours of the morning. "This situation reminds me of the final days at the embassy. The America we once knew doesn't exist anymore."

Sam replied simply, "I hope you're wrong."

Dylan continued to frustrate his enemies. He continued to broadcast, on the move, thanks to help from his friends who supported freedom. "We no longer have a democracy!" Dylan bellowed into his microphone as gunfire erupted in the distance. "Freedom as we once knew it no longer exists! I will continue to broadcast every night from a different location, Martial law cannot stop me!"

The full moon cast an eerie glow across the once-bustling city. Trudy, unable to sleep, sat at Sasha's bedside. She stared aimlessly out the window. A stray dog howled mournfully. A broken shutter slammed against a front porch, trash scattered across the lawn. Jackie, unable to sleep, quietly joined her mother. "I'd like to be able to sleep," Jacked whispered, "but it just feels so weird sleeping in that woman's bedroom. All her stuff in there, it's like she never left!" Trudy nodded understandingly and urged, "Let's go join the guys and see how Steve's doing."

Sam slept in the recliner. Marc sat in the darkness, undetected on the enclosed porch. Occasionally, a military vehicle passed by. Otherwise, the neighborhood seemed empty. Trudy sat on a patio sofa adjacent to Marc, who stared emotionlessly. Trudy stated, "We really can't stay here forever. It's not safe." Marc shrugged.

Following a long moment or two of uncomfortable silence, Marc turned to her and asked, "Where do you suggest we go?"

Trudy responded, "My kids and I haven't seen my sister in Tucson since we entered the witness protection program."

Marc pondered this momentarily and said, "Well, you all are free to go anytime you want, but I question the safety of the open roads. Does Tucson still exist? Is this martial law in place everywhere?"

Trudy stared at him incredulously. "OK, I'll be honest. I'm not sure I trust you. My kids and Steve may think you're Mr. Cool on the College Campus, but I don't! What happened to your wife? Why is Sasha the way she is?"

Marc rubbed his temples, sensing the onset of a nasty migraine. "Oh, I so do not need this shit today!" he bemoaned. "You see I still wear my wedding band? I don't know where the hell she is! As for Sasha, I'm not a fucking shrink! Your guess is as good as mine when it comes to her strange behavior. My gut feeling tells me we need to stick together, at least till we get a handle on this martial law bullshit. What about your husband? Is he still in your life?" Taken back, Trudy fumbled for a response. Annoyed, Marc continued, "Well, you three didn't just land from a spacecraft in my backyard with just the clothing on your backs without good reason. What happened?"

He waited patiently for her reply. Angrily she related some of the events that led her family to become involved in the witness protection program, including her husband and his brother's involvement in excessive gambling, money laundering, and the hit on their mobile home the previous day. "I don't think Adrienne's coming back," he mentioned. "You and Jackie are welcome to take whatever you need from her. Sam and I probably should go for supplies. Steve needs to get stronger before he goes anywhere. We are relatively safe here."

Trudy replied, "Sam has a truck—it's at Gene's Garage for a tune-up. Your Firebird isn't big enough for five adults, one child, and supplies."

Marc nodded in agreement, stating, "We should all have a conversation, preferably at lunch, so we're all on the same page about what's happening."

Marc then napped till Jackie called everyone in to breakfast. All were pleasantly surprised to see Steve at the dining room table, wolfing down waffles and scrambled eggs. "I bounce back quickly," Steve announced.

Marc took his coffee to Sasha's bedroom. He returned moments later. "I want her to sleep as much as she can. Let her play out in the backyard while Sam and I get supplies and get his truck out of the garage."

Trudy frowned. "You're accustomed to being in charge, aren't you?"

Marc finished his coffee and poured a second cup. "Well," he began, "I am a substitute teacher now, and prior to that, as a diplomat, I had to take charge on several matters in the embassy. A lot of the complaining bureaucrat types didn't care for me, and I'm sure you all are aware of how beleaguered the current president is, regardless of whether or not you support his policies."

With that, everyone continued to eat in silence. *Nice, safe political answer,* Trudy surmised, but opted not to respond. Jackie wondered, "Did our president call for this martial law nonsense?" No one knew for sure.

"With this being an election year," Marc opined, "I shouldn't think he'd be in favor of it. Since I'm no longer an ambassador, I can say what I think of any president and his policies. And this president is clueless as to what the U.S. Constitution means! I think we'll learn a bit more, Sam, when we go get your truck and then some supplies." Trudy raised her eyebrows at Marc but said nothing.

Steve mentioned, "I'm feeling better, maybe I can come along, help you guys out?"

Before Marc could reply, Jackie held Steve's hand and stated firmly, "No, absolutely not! At least one day of rest!"

Sam arose from the table and said, "I guess you're grounded, for at least a day, Steve. You know better than to argue with Jackie."

Steve agreed and patted Jackie's hand. Marc turned to Trudy and asked, "Can you please keep an eye on Sasha? We'll be back by midafternoon."

Trudy nodded and requested, "Can you bring some cold medicine? Something for children. I think she may be coming down with a bug. She sure sleeps a lot."

Marc paused and responded, "All right. Oh, and check for news on the radio or TV."

Steve asked, "If this martial law crap is for real, does anyone believe that the mainstream media, state-controlled, will air any truthful news?" No one answered. Marc and Sam turned to go.

Once outside, Marc tossed Sam the keys to the Firebird and donned his leather jacket. "You OK, man?" Sam asked as they got into the car.

Marc replied, "I sure am. Just want to have my hands free in case…" his voice trailed as he displayed a handgun. Sam started to respond but elected not to, and the two drove uptown, surveying the scene.

FREE UNDER SIEGE

Sam and Marc did not converse at all during the short drive through town to Gene's Garage. Anger flashed across Sam's face when he first saw the 1967 Lincoln. A soldier in a brown uniform with a red armband stood guard over the classic. Finding this odd, Marc whispered as he parked his Firebird, "Don't let on you know that vehicle. Let's just get your truck back and go get some supplies." Sam nodded silently as they both entered Gene's shop.

Gene, a kindly gentleman in his midseventies, had been in business over fifty years. "I was beginning to think you weren't coming in," he joked. "I'm not too busy these days since the government started regulating how much an old guy can work. Social security isn't social, and it sure as hell ain't secure!" Sam paid Gene, accepted the keys to his truck, and thanked him.

They turned to go, but Marc lingered momentarily and asked, "Gene, what's up with that wannabe Nazi out there by that Lincoln?"

A look of fear engulfed Gene's craggy features. He replied, "He's been hanging around a couple days. The guy who owned that Lincoln looked like a thug straight out of the movies! They had a spat, and the Nazi shot him!"

Sam commented quietly, "At least there's still a bit of justice." Marc stared at him, and he continued, "That thug burned our home down and killed Dad and Fat Eddie. We were in the witness prot program."

Gene walked with them to the door and advised, "You guys be careful!" He then looked directly at Marc and added, "I mean it, Professor! I remember what you were like when your pops gave you that Firebird, before you went to be an ambassador to whatever fucked-up third world country." Marc shook hands with Gene, assured him that he'd toned it down a lot since Sasha was born. Gene nodded and locked the door behind them.

The soldier was nowhere to be seen as Sam and Marc walked to their respective vehicles. "I'm going over to the shopping center," Marc said, pointing across the street.

Sam replied, "Yeah, I'll meet you over there in a few. Gotta gas up this beast."

Surprisingly, the shopping center's parking lot was empty, with the exception of two young ladies standing beside a parked car. They were obviously in some sort of distress, so Marc steered his Firebird next to them and stopped. "Everything OK, ladies?" he inquired. They seemed frantic. Marc got out, motioned them to pop open the hood, and surveyed the engine. "I'm not much of a mechanic, ladies," he stated earnestly, "but I can see some wires have been cut."

The women screamed horrifically. Marc slammed the hood shut and yelled, "What the fuck?" A soldier clamped his hand on Marc's shoulder and spun him around. "Not too swift, asshole," Marc seethed, "putting your hands on me!" His first punch landed squarely on the soldier's jaw, staggering him against an empty storefront window. Marc grabbed the twenty-something recruit by his hair and slammed his face against the window. The young man crumpled to the sidewalk, semiconscious and bleeding.

"Lucky for you, punk, that it's shatterproof glass!" Marc sneered as he took the soldier's weapon and radio. After tossing the items on the Firebird's backseat. he then noticed a swastika armband on the soldier's right arm. "You twisted, fucking bastard!" he raged as her ripped the armband from his uniform. "Have you any clue what that shit stands for?" The soldier struggled to try to stand, but Marc bitch-slapped him then kicked him in his stomach.

Sam raced over and pulled him away. "I think he's had enough!" Sam declared.

Marc retorted, "You never can be sure with these Nazi bastards!"

Exasperated, Sam added, "We came for supplies, OK?"

Sam consoled the ladies, while Marc used the soldier's handcuffs to cuff him to a nearby empty bicycle rack. To add insult, Mark jumped a garbage can filled with litter on the beaten, bloody soldier. Shaking his head, Sam related, "He's not normally like this, I can tell you for sure. My sister had him for a government class at the college."

One woman whispered, "Well, the soldier did put his hand on him and spun him around!" Marc quickly calmed himself and opened the hood of the women's vehicle. Sam peered under it to assess the problem. "If you don't mind me towing it to Marc's house," he began, "I can fix it. There's an auto parts store near Gene's garage."

Marc nodded in agreement and added, "You are welcome to stay at my place as long as you need to. We have a full house, but it's a lot safer than a motel." The two women looked at each other and then introduced themselves as Jenny and Sara. They opted to ride with Sam and watched apprehensively while he attached a tow chain. Marc said, "I'll put my Firebird in the garage. I'm stopping off at the market. I'll wait at the gate for you all. I'd prefer none of us park in the street, with the solders and all."

Everyone arrived at lunchtime without further incident. Sasha took a liking to Jenny and Sara, much to Marc and Trudy's surprise. "I think she's begun to cope with whatever happened with her nanny," Trudy confided to Marc privately.

He agreed, "Yes, and from here on out, none of us can ever go out alone." He related to her some parts of the incident with the soldier.

Trudy, horrified, gasped, "How savage! Are you always so violent?"

Marc explained, "The soldier put his hands on me, I just defended myself!"

Trudy nodded and prepared a salad for lunch.

Sam introduced Jenny and Sara to Jackie and Steve. Jackie showed them to the guest room. Sam returned to the driveway to work on their car. Marc went out to the patio to start the grill. Sasha played with her dolls near her jungle gym. Steve joined Marc at the grill and stated quietly, "The ladies shouldn't travel at night once Sam gets their car fixed." He looked at Steve inquisitively, who continued, "Yes. I saw some news on TV after you guys left. Every major city in America is under martial law, according to the president. Complete with a ten p.m. curfew."

Marc, thoroughly disgusted, replied, "I'm not surprised. The president has taken his cue from third world nations. Criticize his sorry ass and you get squelched—all in the name of national security. No one has stopped Dylan from broadcasting yet."

Steve said nothing, and Marc left him to handle the grilling. He grabbed a couple of Pepsis and walked around the front to see how Sam was faring with the auto repairs. Soldiers marched by the gate. Marc stared reservedly at them. Sam slid out from beneath the car to drink his Pepsi and observe. "I think the ladies should stay overnight. I'll be finished soon, but it's not safe to travel at night." Marc agreed and related the news accounts heard by the others earlier that day. "There may come a point where we may not be safe in our hometown," he added. "We don't know exactly how many troops are enforcing this martial law."

Everyone ate hungrily by the time Marc returned to the patio. Sasha surprised them by eating two cheeseburgers. She chatted happily with Jackie. Jackie said, "She's doing quite well!"

Sam joined them for dessert. The discussion centered on the soldiers. Jenny and Sara exchanged worried looks. "You're welcome to stay as long as you like," Marc offered. "This house is pretty secure. Us guys are taking turns keeping watch overnight. We'd know if any of those damned soldiers tries to enter."

Steve wondered, "What would you do, Marc, if they do break into this house?"

Marc smiled knowingly and responded, "I'd enjoy the art of self-defense!" Sam shook his head and laughed. Marc added, "Enjoy dessert, I'll eat mine later. I'm going to take a nap so I'll be refreshed to take the first watch tonight. I didn't like the way some of those soldiers watched Sam fix the car." With that having been imparted to their overall apprehensiveness, he retired to his favorite recliner.

The city's inhabitants, gripped with fear, remained in their homes following the sunset curfew. Most listened for Dylan's broadcasts, which aired less frequently due to the more powerful state-supported satellites. The president ordered all independent television stations to cease operations.

No one knew Dylan's whereabouts. The mayor posted his status as "a dissident wanted for questioning." That effectively ended his tenure at the community college. Students registered quietly for classes; the atmosphere was somber. Soldiers' presence on campus was subtle yet intimidating, especially at the apartment complex adjacent to the college.

Rumors abounded of nightly arrests. The mayor declared proudly, "Our city is safe! Criminals no longer roam the streets! The curfew is effective!" The brown-uniformed recruits marched proudly past the podium. He continued, "We can thank our president for these initiatives. His fine leadership deserves reelection to a second term! I—"

The mayor whirled to the sound of a booming broadcast of unknown origin. "Do not listen to the mayor!" Dylan shouted. "He does not want us to have freedom! Both he and this president trampled all over the U.S. Constitution, and they are unfit to hold public office! Vote them both out this fall. Sector 9 is an illegal detainment camp ordered by the president and approved by the mayor!"

The mayor raged to his security staff, "Find that SOB and bring him to me! This has to stop!" Residents cheered wildly for Dylan, and the mayor ordered the police to disburse the crowd with pepper spray.

Everyone ate dessert throughout Dylan's broadcast. Sam finished first and pushed his plate to the center of the table. Sasha played a card game with Jackie at the opposite end of the table, oblivious to the brevity of Dylan's announcement. Sam turned to Jenny and Sara, advising, "I really think you both should stay overnight so you'll have a whole day for travel. It's not going to be safe, especially after dark, for two women alone on a road trip."

Jenny and Sara agreed. "If we leave at sunrise, we should be able to reach Cedar Rapids by late afternoon," Sara stated.

THE EQUINOX NIGHTMARE

Jenny added, "Our families must be worried sick!"

Marc, restless, dozed fitfully in the recliner. Memories of the twelfth-grade U.S. history since 1945 crowded his subconscious, his classmates' taunts about his speech of the Kennedy assassination. The teacher even reported him to the school nurse and the guidance counselor.

Crowds lined the streets of the motorcade route, eager to get a glimpse of the president and Mrs. Kennedy. Marc pushed through onlookers near the book depository and scrambled up flights of stairs.

"Put down the rifle, you sorry son of a bitch!" he screamed at Oswald when he burst through the door. He felt the sucker punch to the left side of his jaw as he attempted to lunge at Lee Harvey Oswald. Two sets of hands roughly hoisted him to his feet, and a harsh, stern voice barked, "You should have stayed in your own time, Marc, you dumb ass! Always thought you could save the world, change history!" Marc broke free of the thugs' grasp and lunged at the thirty-fifth president's assassin. "No, you bastard!" he shouted.

When Marc regained consciousness, he found himself sprawled on his living room floor. Jackie applied an ice pack to a sizeable lump on his forehead. Sam, Steve, and the women gathered nearby, exchanging nervous glances. Sam asked, "Exactly what the hell happened in here?" Fortunately, Sasha was playing outdoors with her dollhouse.

Marc related the events of his recurring nightmare. Jenny and Sara fled to the guest room to gather their belongings. Sam and Steve followed them. "Way to go, ace," Trudy said. "They probably think you're high!" Marc said nothing and struggled to his feet. He sipped from a water bottle and announced, "I'll be OK, no need to worry!"

Several minutes later, Sara and Jenny returned with their personal belongings and said their good-byes to all. "We can make it to my parents' place by sunset," Sara declared confidently. "Thanks for fixing the car, Sam!" They hurried to their car. Marc moved quietly to the window, parted the curtain, and watched as the gate opened to allow the women to pass and then close. Within seconds, an unmarked government car with two occupants followed the college coeds.

Marc shook his head sadly and closed the curtain. "I expect that this will be normal from now on. A lot of surveillance activity, being watched, you know?" Steve and Sam did not respond.

Jackie turned on the television and calmly stated, "Marc, those women were scared of you." Jackie added, "We're used to you, from school and all. You're a bit eccentric. But that stuff about time travel, back to 1963, well, that creeps people out sometimes."

Marc nodded, reflecting on her statement. "I can understand what you're saying," he began, "but it's bizarre why it has become a recurring nightmare."

Everyone turned their attention to the television. A state news broadcaster proudly proclaimed government agents had destroyed a radio station, presumably one having been operated by Dylan. Disgusted, Sam stated, "We need to find Dylan! He'd be safer with us!"

Marc tossed him the keys to his Firebird. "Take Steve with you. It's not safe to be out and about alone."

The women joined them. Trudy complained, "I don't like this! It's dangerous!"

Marc retorted, "Well, if they find Dylan and bring him here, I say that he's more than welcome to broadcast his program from this house! The first soldier that breaks in, I will scatter his brains all over the fucking wall!" Angrily the women left the room and returned to the kitchen. Sam and Steve started for the door. Marc brooded alone in the living room, sipping herbal tea to calm his nerves. The news broadcaster seemed arrogant as he related government-scripted details of the radio station's demolition. He turned off the TV when the president aired a commercial touting his alleged achievements in national security these past four years. *What a fucking hose bag*, he thought as he stood and walked out onto the front porch. The late summer sun set behind a row of vacant homes.

Sam steered the Firebird onto the college campus's athletic department parking lot. The football coach appeared edgy and irritable as he answered questions of two soldiers. Sam continued on to the student lot. Steve marveled at the car's mint condition. "I'm shocked he'd let you drive his car!" Sam shrugged and replied, "I don't know, with his state of mind being what it is, I'm sure he realized that he'd stand out here. We blend in." They returned to town. Soldiers roughly marched two teens out of a convenience store and shoved them into a military van. "Where the hell would Dylan hide?" Steve wondered aloud. Sam stopped at the convenience store.

Steve opted to remain in the car, poring over Marc's eclectic musical tastes. Sam wanted to speak with the clerk, whom he recognized from the college. The clerk behaved skittishly upon Sam's entry into the store. "Chill, I'm not here to rob the place!" Sam joked.

The clerk, Billy, whispered nervously, "I know why you're here, man. Soldiers are always coming in here, asking about you, Steve, and that goofball who subbed at school. Government class, I think it was. Anyway, some soldier got the shit kicked out of him not too long ago."

Sam smiled knowingly, paid for two energy drinks, and asked, "Have you seen Dylan around?" Billy paled instantly. He pointed to the soldiers who stood by the gas pumps and declined to answer. Sam nodded and turned to go.

Once out in the car, Steve asked, "What was all that about? I could see from here that Billy looked like he wanted to puke!"

Sam handed him an energy drink and stated, "Dylan is hiding nearby. Billy is scared of those soldiers. When I back out, I am going to block the soldiers' view of that Dumpster. Open it, act like you're tossing some trash. Call out to Dylan—quietly." Sam casually watched the soldiers as Steve opened the Dumpster. "Dylan!" Steve called out. "It's us, me and Sam! It's OK, we're crashing at Marc's." Dylan peered out from behind the Dumpster. Steve continued, "Hurry up, man!" The soldiers turned and walked slowly toward the store. Dylan scampered to the backseat, tossed his knapsack in, and ducked down as he clambered in. Steve got back in and Sam steered the Firebird away from the soldiers, who now chattered excitedly on their radios. Dylan stayed down on the backseat floor and whispered, "Sam, how'd you guys figure out where I was?"

Sam laughed and turned onto a side street, avoiding a convoy of soldiers. "Oh, just the way Billy reacted in the store. I knew then that you'd been in there. Those soldiers sure are interested in you!"

Steve chuckled and added, "Must be that top-rated radio show you host every day!"

The trio arrived at Marc's within minutes. Steve walked over to test the gate to be certain it had locked. Marc stood in the garage as it automatically opened and stepped outside to allow Sam to park the car inside. A soldier passed by and glared at Marc.

Marc stepped closer to the locked gate as the garage door slowly closed behind him. Other soldiers joined the one who watched Steve. Marc motioned Steve to move away from the locked gate. "You have no business whatsoever here!" he barked at the soldiers. "I suggest you move on, *now*!"

The commanding officer grasped the gate and shouted, "We want to search this house!"

Marc retorted, "Fuck you, asshole! Diplomatic immunity here, shithead!"

Once inside, Steve asked, "For real? You got diplomatic immunity?"

Sam and Dylan appeared from the kitchen. Marc said simply, "No, not anymore. Sounded good, though." Dylan shook his head, quietly putting his knapsack on the floor.

The men gathered on the front porch. A full moon cast eerie shadows on soldiers passing by the gate. Gravely concerned, Dylan whispered, "Is it safe here?"

Marc stared aimlessly at the soldiers and replied, "I believe so, at least for the time being."

News broadcast became more grim. The women questioned the safety aspect; government-sanctioned troops slowly increased. Townspeople were commanded by the mayor via the federal government to obey a dusk curfew or face arrest and incarceration. Dylan fumed but remained silent.

Sasha joined everyone in the living room, causing Marc to weigh his words carefully. "If we can just make it through the fall," he began, "there's hope we'll elect a new president in November."

Dylan stared at him incredulously and replied, "Are you insane? There are soldiers everywhere! People will be too scared to go to the polls! It'll be such a crock, no one will believe the outcome!"

Everyone agreed with Dylan. Marc picked up his daughter and held her tightly. She whined, "Are we going to have to move again, Daddy?"

Marc answered, "I don't know yet." He carried her upstairs and tucked her into bed. After turning off her light, he parted the curtain slightly, only to notice an unmarked van parked across the street, occupied by two soldiers. Marc rejoined the others and reported his discovery.

Trudy, agitated, stated adamantly, "Marc, you need to think of your daughter! This is not a fit environment for any child!" Marc pondered the comments and responded sarcastically, "Would you rather I just kill every soldier? Come on, you already think I'm unstable! You practically said that once about Sasha!"

Sam intervened. "This isn't going to get us anywhere. We have to make some decisions *soon*!" Steve and Jackie agreed. Dylan refused to speak, still irate.

Dylan's anger dissipated immediately upon seeing the television screen flash brightly. A state-supported news broadcast followed. "Martial law will be strictly enforced at all times," the announcer began amid images of downtown looters being beaten and arrested. "Curfew will be enforced strictly, without exception! In an unrelated matter of national interest, the president has lost a recall election. The general has assumed full powers, per executive order—"

Horror-struck, Trudy turned off the television.

Marc parted the living room curtain slightly and watched as convoys of soldiers motored past. "At some point, we are going to have to leave here, find supplies and shelter elsewhere. My cousin Joel lives in a gated community. He's a big believer in the Second Amendment, no shortage of weaponry, for sure." Everyone looked at one another, speechless. Marc continued, "At some point, we may need to defend ourselves. One pistol and two boxes of bullets won't cut it!"

Dylan paced the room and responded, "Well, depending upon how long it takes to get there, we can stop at the Pig Lady's farm. She might help us, if you like to barter?"

Sasha absorbed much of the adults' conversation. "No, this is *not* another shopping trip," Marc said as he scooped her up and carted her off to her room. "It is now your bedtime!" Moments later, he returned to announce simply, "We must make a plan if we are to succeed in the safety of Cousin Joel's."

UNDER ENEMY ATTACK

Marc rejoined the group once Sasha had fallen asleep. Sam asked, "Is your cousin Joel pretty stable? I mean, we really know nothing about him." Steve nodded in agreement.

Marc looked confident, in good humor. "Aside from when he goosed my wife, Ginny, at an embassy Christmas party a few years ago, he's mostly a rather eccentric individual."

Trudy and Jackie exchanged nervous glances. Noticing this, Marc continued, "Oh, he's harmless. The wealthy ol' bastard never had a wife or kids to spend money on, so he'd just act a bit outrageously. I think we need to plan to leave soon, before those damn soldiers raid this house!" He patted a pistol that he'd tucked in his belt. "We must be prepared to defend ourselves!"

Dylan spoke up. "I hate to admit it," he argued, "but he's absolutely right. Have we forgotten what happened to my radio broadcasts from the college? This is *not* a fucking democracy anymore! Sam, you need to be prepared to use that pistol Marc gave you when you and Steve rescued me from that convenience store. Marc, as goofy as I think you are, I am certain that you know how to fight."

Marc opened his jacket, displaying his weapon. Dylan nodded; Trudy interrupted, "I don't like this!" she shrieked. "Who are you, Marc? Really?"

Dylan raised his hand and cautioned, "It is necessary."

Marc asked, "Are you aware of Sector 9, Trudy? Our idiot mayor has no issue with free people being enslaved! I dealt with this sort of shit when I finished my career as an ambassador. The mayor is simply a common puppet. No doubt he reports to the one they refer to as the commandant."

Dylan stated, "Damn! You're not that goofy after all! A ruse for the college kids?" Marc opted to ignore the remarks. Gunfire echoed in the distance. All reacted nervously except Dylan and Marc.

"It's not going to get any better," Marc stated sadly. Dylan peeked out the window. Tanks in formation slowly rumbled past. "It's changed, never going to be like it used to be. We need to load as many supplies as possible into Sam's truck and my Firebird. We aren't going to be safe here much longer." Dylan suggested Trudy ride with Marc and Sasha, to offer the inference of a family traveling.

Trudy decided to check on Sasha, while the others carefully packed the supplies. "I think we can reach Joel's in no more than two days. We have to stick together," Marc directed.

Dylan added, "It'll be a challenge, but we can do this! Before my radio station was destroyed by this occupation, I learned of various factions, teams fighting for constitutional freedoms. They are mostly in rural locales."

A dense fog engulfed the city. Steve stood on the porch now, watching Sam and Jackie pack the truck. Marc backed his Firebird onto the front lawn, providing clear passage for Sam's truck. Marc stood by his car, silently observing the soldiers who marched beside the tanks. He joined Steve on the porch, questioning, "Are you up for this, man?" Steve is asleep.

"Please don't tell me that you'll be carrying a gun!" Trudy pleaded.

Marc replied, "If it makes you feel any better, I've attached a silencer to my gun."

She turned and walked to Sam and Jackie. Jackie tried to console her mother. "It has to be this way, Mom," Sam stated calmly. "We have to be able to protect ourselves."

With that, Sam secured the load, and they followed Marc and Steve back into the house. All agreed to rest for several hours; they planned to leave at daybreak, regardless of the fog. "It may work to our advantage," Dylan announced. "The soldiers expect us to leave through the front gate. We go out the back, cut through the neighbor's yard."

Marc liked Dylan's plan, and offered, "Hell yeah, and I'll set this house on fire! That'll give these damned communist bastards a wake-up call!" Trudy and Jackie appeared apprehensive. Marc settled into his favorite recliner for a short nap. The fog dissipated only slightly by daybreak. Sam quietly moved the vehicles to the backyard gate. Marc carried a sleeping Sasha to the Firebird. Trudy assisted in getting her settled in the backseat. Everyone watched as Marc ran back inside, wondering what he may have forgotten. Marc doused the living room furniture with gasoline and backed into the kitchen, at the point in which all power had been cut. He heard the front gate open, followed by incessant ranting by Russian soldiers. Emptying the gas on the back porch, he tossed a match and sped to the Firebird, which now idled.

Trudy checked on Sasha, still asleep, and watched aghast at the quickly spreading blaze. Marc hopped into the car and soon caught up to Sam, who had opted to pass through three neighboring backyards to escape detection.

Once on the main highway, Marc stayed within sight of Sam's taillights. The fog began to dissipate. Trudy paused then asked, "Was that really necessary, setting the house on fire? Really, you do have a way of attracting attention!" Marc laughed and said nothing. He turned on the radio, hoping to hear news.

The morning news was not at all promising. "The president has lost the election," the reporter stated solemnly, "and the commandant has immediately assumed power. His first order of business has been to issue an executive order dissolving all agencies of government, with exceptions being defense and finance. Excess personnel will be transferred to specific work installations."

Marc heard enough. "So do you still think this is a free country, babe?" Trudy glared, pointing as Sam turned into Gene's Garage. He watched, puzzled, as all activity had ceased.

The 1967 Lincoln remained on the side lot. Sam and Steve walked to it, talking quietly among themselves. Marc parked by the gas pumps and confronted them. "What gives? We really need to stay on the move!"

Unhappily Sam replied, "This car belongs to the asshole who killed my dad and my uncle. We were in witness protection."

Marc opened the driver's side door, shocked to find pools of blood throughout the car. "Whoever owned this car, Sam," he said calmly, "in all likelihood, is dead. This much blood—he couldn't have survived long!" After glancing back at Trudy, he added, "We really need to get going. The fog will lift soon, and we must put some serious distance from this damned city!" They filled their gas tanks and went inside to see if they could find useful items.

The eerie silence unnerved both Sam and Marc. "Sam, we can't let this bother us. Nothing will ever be like it was before, so it's basically gut check time!" Sam nodded, filled a small bag with snacks, and started back to his truck. Marc doused the newspaper rack with lighter fluid, lit it, and ran to his car.

Steve and Jackie turned to watch as Gene's Garage soon burned brightly. Sam increased his speed, pleasantly surprised to see Marc keeping approximately one car length behind. Jackie mused, "He's got quite a fetish for fire, hasn't he?"

Steve caressed her hand and opined, "I think he's making it personal. Maybe he's sending a message to the commandant."

Marc thoroughly enjoyed this; he felt truly reenergized. Trudy gazed at him and questioned, "Are you out of your mind? Just what are you trying to prove?" A sly smile crossed Marc's face. Trudy continued to question him. "Is there something wrong with you? Sometimes, you remind me of that thug who killed my husband and his brother!"

Marc gazed evenly at her, debating whether or not to respond. With an impish grin, he replied, "Oh, hell, I hope not. I never knew your husband or his brother-in-law, but I certainly hope I have enough gumption to behave and not land my ass in the witness protection program!" Trudy was furious. "Yes, dear, I talked to Sam back at the garage. We have to stick together, the seven of us, if we are to make it to Joel's in one piece!"

Sam turned suddenly onto a long drive, which led up to a farmhouse, seemingly abandoned. "What the fuck?" Marc muttered as he turned to follow him. Sasha stirred on the backseat. Trudy glared at him. Marc stopped the car and got out to see what was happening with Sam, Jackie, Dylan, and Steve.

"Jackie and Steve needed to use the bathroom," Sam explained. "Friends of ours live here. Or used to, by the looks of things."

Disgusted, Marc stated, "We can't be stopping every hour, man! We need to put some fucking distance between ourselves and the city!" Steve and Jackie returned to the truck. Sam nodded, and the three started up the lane. Marc walked quickly to the Firebird and turned the ignition as a dusty, beat-up Dodge Charger with two twenty-ish males drove up alongside, narrowly missing his door. Marc pressed down on his automatic window and snarled, "I hope you have a good reason for pulling a shit-for-brains stunt like that!"

The driver lit a cigarette and replied, "We heard about people like y'all—freedom fighters. We want to go with you!'

Marc eyed the two carefully. Something was off about them, he felt. "I'm afraid that's not an option," he began. "I don't know you." The passenger slowly moved his arm along the console. Marc quickly drew his gun and fired two shots, one in each man's forehead, killing them instantly. "Still think I'm a thug?" he asked Trudy, who trembled. Sasha woke up; Trudy turned to shield her. "I'm a high-class thug," he joked. "I believe in using a silencer!" Gesturing at Sasha, he added, "She doesn't understand any of this. We cannot relax till we get to Joel's."

Trudy had no comment, and within several minutes, they had caught up to Sam. They drove for approximately ten more miles. The fog had dissipated entirely. Sasha pointed at a fenced-in facility. "Is that a jail, Daddy?" she asked. Marc and Trudy watched as uniformed people walked aimlessly, while many toiled in gardens. "Looks like some sort of work camp," Marc said. Sasha stared as sad faces gazed sadly at them through the chain-link fence. Then she began to color in her book.

Staying off main highways made for a longer journey, but everyone agreed it was necessary, to lessen the risk of contact with soldiers. Shortly after 1:00 p.m., they stopped for a lunch break in a small town's park, Happy Trails. Marc and Sam stood watch, guns drawn. Dylan joined them, handing each a Pepsi. "What exactly happened back there, Marc? Took you a little while to catch up."

Marc shook his head and replied, "It's best not to talk about it. I did what needed to be done. I only hope we don't get into a situation where we are outnumbered."

Dylan pulled out a map and studied it. "If we can find a safe area to camp tonight, with a sunrise start tomorrow, we should reach your cousin's sometime after lunch." Marc nodded in agreement. Dylan rejoined the others.

Sam waited till he was out of hearing range and asked, "Did you have to kill again?"

Stoically Marc responded, "Yes."

Both stared skyward. The sun shone brightly. Marc sensed that Sam wanted to say more. "Sam," he began, "I don't like this any more than you do. We really must fight to stay alive! I want to believe it'll be fine once we get to Joel's."

Steve brought them a plate and joined the conversation. "Everything OK, guys?" he asked.

Sam and Marc wolfed down sandwiches and chips. "Killing people gives me an appetite," Marc stated sarcastically. Steve raised an eyebrow.

"He ran into trouble back at that farmhouse is all," Sam informed him. "I just wish there didn't have to be so much bloodshed!"

Marc finished his Pepsi, belched, and responded, "Well, I don't get my jollies from shooting people, if that's what you're implying. As for the fires, it helps slow down any soldiers pursuing us. If you think we're still a free people, talk to Dylan. I'm sure that the commandant just wanted to have him over for a cup of tea!"

Dylan rejoined them, waving the map. "The ladies want to know where we'll camp tonight."

Marc pointed at a location approximately two hundred miles to the northwest. "Sasha's nanny had an aunt in a rest home, the Shady

THE EQUINOX NIGHTMARE

Rest, I think it's called. We visited there several times. The administrator is a real government hack, but the caretaker, Duke, farms the land. All the residents enjoy fresh vegetables. He is a real survivalist. I'm sure we can buy more ammo from him."

The men finished their conversation and returned to speak with the women. Marc picked up his daughter and held her high. She laughed. "Put me down, Daddy, you are just being so silly!"

The others glanced at one another. Sam whispered in his mother's ear, "He'll be fine." Everyone helped clean up the picnic site and resumed their travel. Driving throughout the countryside proved uneventful, much to everyone's delight. As dusk approached, Marc began to yawn, somewhat tired of driving. Trudy offered to drive, but Marc declined. "We're getting close to where we're going to camp tonight. Shouldn't be much farther." Moments later, Sam turned off onto a gravel road.

Trudy raised her eyebrows. Marc pointed at a clearing in the distance. "Nice plantation-style home," Trudy remarked.

Marc added, "Yeah, it's the assisted living facility that Adrienne's aunt still lives in. I know the maintenance guy, Duke. He was preparing for this martial law crap when Sasha, Adrienne, and I visited here. Duke said that he owned all the land surrounding the home. We can camp there anytime we're visiting." Sam parked his truck. They all climbed out and approached the Firebird.

"So this is where we camp for the night?" Dylan asked. Marc nodded, got out of his car, and turned to pluck Sasha from the backseat.

Steve added, "Can we build a fire here? It's already getting chilly!"

"OK," Marc responded. "I don't think anyone should go very far into those woods alone to gather firewood. Sam and I have the only weapons, so we have to only use them in extreme situations. I'll take first watch." Sam and Steve grabbed flashlights and started off to gather wood. Dylan and Marc talked quietly, while the women helped Sasha into her sleeping bag. Then Jackie prepared a snack.

"We're sitting ducks out here!" Dylan related.

Marc disagreed. "We're all right as long as we stay off the main highways. Sure, it'll take longer to reach Cousin Joel's, but we've avoided the troops so far. I don't think the government has seized control of the farmland just yet."

Dylan held the map to his flashlight. "We will have to cross one state-maintained highway tomorrow in order to reach your cousin Joel's. How do we avoid troops?"

Marc leaned on his Firebird and replied, "We'll find a way to deal with it, if and when it occurs."

Duke settled back into the porch swing, having finished assisting the residents in retiring for the night. When the campers built the fire, he raised his night vision goggles and smiled knowingly. Freedom fighters always elevated his mood. He patted his modified shotgun fondly.

The administrator's shrill voice disrupted the tranquility of the evening. "You need to register that weapon with the central weapons department!" he barked. "Or else the commandant's troops will come for you!"

Duke gently placed the barrel of his gun against the administrator's temple and stated stoically, "Go back to your state-supported apartment, Ted. You're a pampered, overbearing pip-squeak of an ass! But if you even think of ratting me out to your Nazi goon hacks, I'll scatter what few brains you have all over this lawn. And then, I'll feed what's left of you to the hogs, assuming you don't give them indigestion!" Ted whimpered slightly and left the grounds without further incident. Duke watched him go and thought that rank amateur had no clue how many weapons and how much ammo he had stored throughout the assisted living facility. Hell, even some of the stronger, healthier residents had taken shooting lessons!

While the others enjoyed snacks, Marc tied ropes to trees lining the entrance to their campsite. When a full moon appeared, he tied empty cans to the makeshift alert system. Damn, he felt exhausted all of a sudden. He rejoined the others briefly then assisted Sasha into her sleeping bag. Trudy and Jackie watched, saying nothing.

Once Sasha drifted off to sleep, he began the first watch. Everyone else gathered around the fire and talked quietly. He sat on the trunk of his Firebird, his flashlight and gun within easy reach. He tapped the silencer with his index finger and gazed at the starlit night. A full moon, everything so serene, it just didn't seem like martial law and all the subsequent events should have occurred.

Steve approached, shuffling in the gravel. "Just making some noise," he joked. "Don't want to get shot!" Marc did not speak. Steve continued, "Not to get in your business, man, but, like, are you OK? I mean, you're like, the leader of our group." In the pale moonlight, he tried to detect Marc's facial expression, which appeared cold and without emotion.

Marc looked directly at Steve, stating emphatically, "Your girlfriend's mother thinks I enjoy killing people."

Unprepared for such blunt speech, he fumbled for a response. Marc toyed with his gun's silencer. "A marine gave me this as we were being run out of our embassy. There was no democracy whatsoever in that country also. Trudy needs to realize that now, it is survival of the fittest. In order for us to reach my cousin Joel's estate in one piece, we must *all* be on the same page."

Steve asked, "Anything I can do to help keep us safe?"

Marc sighed, pondering his response carefully. "I'll speak to the group at daybreak, but I have a plan in mind for you and Dylan. You're going to meet Duke—he is the maintenance man, caretaker, whatever his title is—at that elderly assisted living facility up yonder." Marc pointed at the fields at the back of the home. "He and his family have farmed that land for generations. They are one of a very few family farms that our joke of a government hasn't been able to seize. We'll be able to get freshwater, and I plan to ask him to teach you and Dylan to shoot. Duke keeps the rats out of his corn crib with a WWII sniper rifle!"

Taken aback just a bit, Steve simply replied, "Damn! You sure know some colorful individuals!"

Marc nodded, and continued, "I certainly do. We met Duke when we visited Adrienne's aunt there some time ago, before I became ambassador. Duke predicted a lot of what has happened in our country since we were last here. Sad to say, most people didn't believe him. Hell, man, try to get some sleep. We need everyone to be as well rested as possible."

Duke continued to watch the group through his night vision goggles, most pleased to see Marc, Sasha, and the others. He sipped a Pepsi and patted his modified rifle lovingly. Sam and Steve woke Marc from a sound sleep at approximately two in the morning. "Not bad," Marc laughed. "For once I slept normally!" He walked to the campfire, added some wood, and grabbing a blanket, curled up next to his daughter. He found the night breeze most relaxing. Trudy and Jackie slept well; Dylan did not. An hour after Sam and Steve began their watch, Dylan joined them, shared his concerns of Joel, martial law, and the assisted living facility.

"We are sitting ducks out here," Dylan opined. "That assisted living place is out in the middle of nowhere! Soldiers can roll in at any time!"

Steve and Sam weren't worried. Sam replied, "All Marc wants to do here is visit people he knows. It's not like we're going to stay long."

Steve added, "Besides, the women will want to freshen up, and we might be able to get a good breakfast!" Dylan relented and walked around their campsite before crawling into his sleeping bag.

Duke now slept with his modified rifle by his bedside. He listened to the nightly government broadcast and sensed trouble on the horizon, especially following his earlier exchange with Ted. Well, he surmised, if any soldiers tried to seize his family's land, there'd be hell to pay! Good thing several residents had taken him up on his shooting lessons. If it came down to it, he'd gladly put a bullet in Ted's fat ass!

The sunrise, accompanied by a glorious blue sky, elevated the campers' moods. Quickly and quietly everyone loaded their belongings. Marc extinguished the campfire and disposed of the stringed cans. They drove to the assisted living facility without incident.

Duke stood on the porch, greeting the travelers warmly. "Welcome! It's been a long time, Marc! Glad to see you're out of that nonsense with the embassy, although what has happened to our country is a hell of a lot worse!" The two men shook hands, and Marc introduced the group. Duke tipped his hat and offered a suggestion, "Y'all put your wheels out back, by my barn, so you can't be seen from the road." Steve accepted Marc's keys and followed Sam to move the vehicles.

Marc sighed and mentioned, "Yeah, I don't miss that embassy. Damn near didn't make it out."

Duke nodded and replied, "I know. Well, all the residents are up having breakfast. I want to check on them. I'll show you ladies to my guest rooms—each with its own bathroom, so y'all can freshen up if you want to, and then join us for breakfast, all right? Steve, I'd like to have a few words with you and Marc, if you don't mind." He waited till the women went in and spoke tersely. "I got a bad feel, gents. Ted, this home's government administrator is a low-down, backstabbing weasel!"

The two stared inquisitively at Duke. "Yeah, that damn Nazi regime in what used to be our nation's capital up and decided to appoint an administrator to oversee our family's business. I heard tell it's like that everywhere." Marc couldn't argue that point.

Steve asked, "What's that got to do with us?"

Duke turned to him and laughed. "Well, you seven folks are celebrities! That Nazi, the commandant, wants you guys hung right alongside Dylan! According to their propaganda, you all are now enemies of the state. Damn, I like your style! We just better stay on alert and be ready for anything!" They joined the others in the large dining room.

While the others enjoyed a hearty country-style breakfast prepared by the cook, Mame, Marc showered and changed clothes. Joining Duke in the kitchen, he accepted a cup of coffee. "You OK?" Duke asked. "You look a mite wore down."

Exasperated, Marc responded, "Oh, it's probably all this shit—Adrienne disappeared. Soldiers got her downtown, I suspect. We're going to my cousin Joel's estate."

Mame burst into the kitchen and stated, "Ms. Jane has wheeled herself out onto the front porch again! She's not eating again and has her husband's gun!"

Duke assured Mame no harm would come to anyone. He and Marc joined Ms. Jane on the porch. Marc noticed that the smell of the magnolias were rather captivating. Duke gestured, "She's Adrienne's aunt. I'll let you talk to her." Marc set his coffee cup on the porch rail and, grabbing a lawn chair nearby, sat next to her in her wheelchair. She gazed intently at the woods.

Marc gently took the gun from her right hand. "That's fine," Jane quietly stated. "I got plenty of ammo in the pouch there." Marc checked and discovered it to be true. "My late husband, Elwen, told me that no Nazi bastard will take us alive, and today is just as good a day to die as any!" Stunned, he could only muster a stare of disbelief.

Duke interrupted, "We got trouble! Check out those woods!" He pointed; soldiers gathered in formation, apparently waiting for instruction. Marc took all the boxes of bullets from Jane's wheelchair pouch and set them on a small table. Duke hollered for Mame, who wheeled Jane to her room. "I hope your people can shoot! We are going to have to defend our position!" Marc finished his coffee and crouched behind a pillar.

TED THE SNITCH

Duke joined Marc on the front porch, brandishing a modified rifle. "This is not going to end well!" he raged.

Marc kept his cool. "Is everyone armed?" he asked.

Duke nodded excitedly. "Hell yeah, even Jackie and Mame! The other woman, Trudy, is holed up with your daughter. Bring it on, you Nazi bastards!"

Gunfire erupted immediately; Marc and Duke lost count of the number of casualties. "I don't think they expected us to be ready," Duke stated. "Maybe now they'll leave us country folk be!"

Marc observed, "I'm not sure it's over. It's too damned quiet for my liking!"

Steve surprised them, calling out, "One of you needs to come inside and check out this shit!"

Duke turned to Marc and said, "You go. I'm not leaving my post. Those bastards may try to get the drop on us! It ain't happening!"

Marc reloaded his gun then backed up inside to the large community room to discover Steve holding Ted, the administrator, at gunpoint. "What the fuck…" Marc's voiced trailed. Ted smirked arrogantly.

Steve prodded him in the back with his shotgun. "Go on," he shouted angrily at Ted, "start talking! How did those fucking soldiers know we were here?"

Marc walked over to them and bitch-slapped Ted. "Well, answer the question, dumb ass!"

Dylan joined them and promptly smacked Ted upside his head. "You heard him, damn it! Answer his question, you asshole!"

Marc pistol-whipped Ted, and the administrator tumbled onto a sofa. Bleeding from his mouth, Ted sputtered, "You don't get it! You so-called freedom fighters never do. It's all about national security and those who'd violate that security! Dylan!"

Dylan started to respond, but Marc raised his gun. "Who the hell are you, Ted, to judge who's a security risk? You're nothing but a hack for that fucking commandant!" Ted crossed his arms and pouted defiantly now.

Marc's patience wore thin. "I will not debate this shit with you, Ted! Plain and simple, did you rat us out to the commandant?" Ted turned up his nose and refused to respond. Marc punched him in his face, causing him to bleed profusely now.

Steve and Jackie joined them. "Sam's covering the back," Steve began. "You ought to see the body count! This is worse than some Western flick!"

Jackie added, "Is beating up the wimp going to really accomplish anything?"

Marc hoisted Ted by his throat against the wall. Ted gasped, "OK, I'll talk!" Marc slammed him into a nearby Hoveround. Ted wiped his face and said, "Yes, I called the commandant. Big bucks for Dylan!"

Marc nodded and began duct-taping Ted to the motorized scooter. "Well, Ted," he decided, "you're not going to collect any of that reward. We're leaving this farm, and Duke will like this, you are going to be the diversion!" Marc smiled slyly as he taped Ted's mouth.

Duke moved quickly, taped Ted's wrists to the scooter armrest, stuffed a dirty shop rag into Ted's mouth, and made several changes to the scooter's program. Marc stepped aside as Duke fiddled with the remote. Dylan, Jackie, and Steve whispered among themselves.

Duke effortlessly pushed Ted to the side porch exit and started the remote; Ted zipped down the handicapped ramp and proceeded out onto the long driveway.

The first shot hit Ted in his right temple; bone fragments and brain matter splattered on the gravel. Marc winced and turned away. Duke cheered raucously, as did Mame and many of the home's residents, who apparently watched from their windows.

The lifeless administrator continued on toward the road. Hidden soldiers fired on on him until he was no longer recognizable. Duke just laughed. "You guys can escape out back while we cover front. There's a dirt road behind the barn—it'll lead you to an unincorporated area. There's a little diner, fortified, and tell them I sent you. They'll help you get onto the back roads again."

Marc protested, "Duke, we can't just up and leave! Those soldiers may move in on you all!"

Duke chuckled. "Most all our residents know how to shoot. And they are quite good. This is our home. We'll defend it to the last man standing!"

Several residents joined them. All brandished weapons. Marc paced around the parlor. Mame brought Sasha to him. Duke gestured confidently. "I think we got it covered," he stated. "No one here can stand the commandant or his Nazi goose-steppers!" Marc nodded, realizing it was futile to argue.

Everyone gathered at the barn. No one spoke as they got into their respective vehicles. Sam nodded confidently as they left the farm. His mother, Trudy, squirmed unhappily in the Firebird. Marc followed Sam off the farm as Trudy stated unhappily, "Is this senseless killing ever going to stop?"

Marc responded in an even tone, "Depends on which side of the gun you're on." Trudy slumped in the backseat and said nothing.

Within a half-hour, they reached the unincorporated area Duke had described. The diner, a rather rustic structure, appeared inviting. "The old town once boasted a population of five hundred," Duke said, "before society went to hell."

Together, Marc and Sam knocked on the diner's door. Pearl's Diner, the faded sign read, advertised home-cooked meals. An elderly woman, petite in stature, opened the door and peered cautiously. "Duke sent us," Marc explained.

Sam added, "There are seven of us. We're almost out of ammo, and we have at least a day of travel to reach Marc's cousin's estate!"

Pearl nodded, stepped around the two, and waved to the others to come inside. Everyone marveled at the decor—1960's rural America. A nickelodeon, a soda fountain, and the booths reminded all of a simpler, less hectic time. Marc briefly reminisced of his older brother having taken him for ice cream sodas and baseball cards at Chuck's Drug Store while their mom worked nights.

"Pay attention!" Pearl snapped. "This is serious business!" Marc wiped a cold sweat from his brow and glanced around the room. Steve and Jackie settled into a booth. Sam and Dylan kept their guns drawn, maintaining a vigil at the diner's entrance. Trudy and Sasha selected stools at the counter. Marc daydreamed about the roast beef plates offered at the five-and-dime stores.

Pearl continued, "Duke sent you, I'm sure. Those soldiers are evil!" She stared directly at Dylan. "They want you, boy! I heard most all your radio broadcasts before State Radio took over." Dylan listened respectfully. "It's never going to be the way it used to be. Those work camps you passed, that's just the tip of the iceberg. Guys like you, Dylan, if captured, are never heard from again!" Trudy shook her head sadly.

While Pearl regaled the group with her dire outlook, a young woman, presumably her granddaughter, Jamie, poured water for those seated. Marc sat at the counter, and Pearl turned her attention on him.

"You, sir, have had a dark, murky past." Marc stirred restlessly. "You were once an ambassador, working to promote agenda of our final president. Yes, we small-town folk had cable television and newspapers."

Jamie added, "Internet too, those who had computers." Pearl nodded patiently. Jamie related, "For those who prepared for this martial law, we are better off than most. Soldiers haven't bothered us because we are self-contained but scattered about where they can't readily find us. Would you have stopped if Duke hadn't told you about us?" Jamie stood next to Pearl and offered her a hug.

Marc started to speak, but Pearl interjected, "You wear a wedding ring, but that woman with your child is *not* your wife! There is darkness in your heart, and you are still haunted—you don't sleep much!"

How the hell does she know all this shit? he wondered. Duke would not talk about him in such a way. Pearl wagged a finger. "Now, hear me clearly on this point! For a very long time, the breakdown slowly occurred. People were more concerned about parties, having more stuff than the neighbors, instead of paying attention to the erosion and disappearance of basic freedom!"

She paused to allow them to contemplate her statements. Dylan nodded in agreement. Marc responded, "I agree 100 percent with you, but now we are all in survival mode. We are headed to my cousin Joel's. He has a secure, gated estate."

Pearl observed, "Yes, the well-to-do have been able to resist all the commandant's directives. At some point, I foresee the sheep in those work camps being trained by the commandant's forces to crush *all* resistance! I may not live long enough to witness it, but that is what I believe."

Marc drank water, replying quietly, "I was told this over thirty years ago, by a WWII veteran, when I was a kid working at McDonald's." Pearl gestured to the group.

Sam, simply fed up with hearing speeches, dismissed Pearl's gesture. "OK, Pearl," he seethed, "so this is all my generation's fault? I don't think so!"

Marc interjected, "Take it easy, man, she wasn't implying that at all! This mess has been a long time in the making."

Steve chimed in, "This isn't really a democracy. If we are to get to Joel's estate in one piece, then we're going to have to work together!"

Pearl beamed proudly. "Now you're talking! I know you'll make it!"

She whistled happily while she packed them a huge picnic lunch. Dylan whispered to Sam, "We are now basically just a carnival of souls on a roller-coaster ride in hopes of getting safely to the fun house, commonly known as Cousin Joel's." Sam started to respond but opted not to. *Does everyone have to be so profound?* he wondered. He and Steve checked for soldiers; the streets remained empty. Everyone piled into their respective rides after thanking Pearl.

The seven freedom seekers pressed on. Their journey, at times, made some feel so alone. They encountered no one during their morning drive. Shortly after noon, they stopped in a rest area to enjoy Pearl's tasty picnic lunch. "We should be at Joel's by dusk," Marc stated between bites of homemade chicken salad sandwiches. "Damn, Pearl must have had quite a crowd in her place!" No one responded. Marc sensed some tension in the group but opted not to address it.

A series of ringing bells echoed in the distance. Everyone quickly finished their lunches and momentarily resumed their travel. After only several miles, they came upon a work camp. Its inhabitants wandered aimlessly in the yard. Marc stopped his car abruptly, ran to the trunk, and retrieved a high-powered rifle and some wire cutters. Sam stopped and stared while Marc began cutting an opening in the fence. The prisoners gathered closely by in an effort to shield the tower guard's view of Marc's action.

The guard spotted the action as the last prisoner escaped through the fence. Marc dropped the wire cutters, picked up his rifle, aimed at the guard, and picked him off with a single shot. The prisoners ran into the woods.

Dylan watched as Marc ran back to the Firebird and gunned its engine. "I can't believe he'd stop and pull shit like this! All it'll do is draw attention to us!"

Jackie stated calmly, "Well, maybe he had a plan. It's possible too that he's sick of seeing our people locked up involuntarily in those damn work camps!"

Sam disagreed. "He is simply out of control. I'm not sure I trust him to get us to safety. I think we need to leave the group before he gets us all killed!"

Steve suggested, "Let's drive till we find a reasonably safe, secluded spot where we can talk this out."

Sam shrugged, replying, "I don't care, my mind is made up. I'm leaving this group! Are you all with me? Take your time, think it over, and give me an answer when we stop again." His passengers simply stared, shocked.

Nothing further occurred as all continued northward. The work camp's alarms sounded an escape, but the noise soon became a distant memory. Approximately an hour later, they reached a crossroad. Sam braked to a halt; Marc stopped his car as well. With the exception of the napping Sasha, everyone gathered around the truck to talk.

"What the hell was that about, back at that work camp?" Sam raged. "Are you trying to get us all killed?"

Marc started to answer, but Dylan interrupted, "You are nuts, man, plain and simple! That stunt may have more government goons on our trail!"

Steve added, "Yeah, we have no confidence in you or your ability to lead!"

Sam said, "We don't want to go with you to your cousin Joel's. We'll take our chances out here."

Marc looked at them all and replied, "OK, go for it. I don't give a fuck what you do!"

Jackie walked and stood next to her mother. "I'm not going with you, Sam. Neither is Mom." She gazed fiercely at Steve. "Do what you want. I can't be with you anymore. We have no life as it is!"

Steve did not expect this at all from his longtime girlfriend. He started to speak, but she cut him off. "No, don't talk to me, just listen. It isn't that I don't love you anymore, because I do. After the president declared martial law, I knew we'd never have the life we planned. Dylan, you're an intelligent guy. But I don't want to be a part of your political fight. Neither does our mom." Sam raised his hand, but she continued, "You're my brother, Sam, not my boss. I am going with Marc and Sasha to Joel's. So is Mom. Go play your rebel freedom fighter games yourselves!" With that, she led her mother back to the Firebird, leaving Marc with the guys.

Marc was taken aback by Jackie's candor. "Well, gentlemen," he began, "the lady has spoken. I suppose this is where we all part ways.

No reason for me to be pissed at you guys, really. Sam, I will keep your mom and sister safe. You got a map. If you change your minds, you all are always welcome at Joel's." He extended his hand, but all refused it, turned, and stormed off.

Marc joined the others in his car. They sat, watching Sam, Steve, and Dylan drive away. Trudy asked, "Will we ever see them again?"

Marc shrugged. "I'm not sure. Sam was pretty pissed."

Sasha started to stir from her nap. Jackie admonished him, "Watch the language, *please*! This is your daughter here!"

Trudy smiled. "Does Joel talk like that?"

Marc started the car and resumed their travel after Sam's truck faded from sight.

"To answer your question," he began, "I don't know. Haven't seen the guy since I was an ambassador. He really loved my wife and stepson. Ginny was pregnant with Sasha at the time." Trudy and Jackie glanced at each other but said nothing. Marc sensed their apprehension and stated, "With a bit of luck and no interruptions, we should be at Joel's by suppertime." Jackie and Sasha played video games. Trudy settled back and sipped coffee from a thermos.

"Pearl's coffee is good," she said. "As is her food." Marc nodded.

Moments later, they stopped in a small town. Marc pulled off to the side of Main Street and stopped to study the map. "Are we lost?" Trudy wondered aloud.

Marc lied, "Of course not. I'm just concerned we may run into soldiers. After we leave this town, we cross a state highway. Just an uneasy feeling I got, is all. I don't want to be in a situation that I have to—our way out of, you know?"

A sudden breeze caused Marc to tremble slightly then sneeze.

"Are you OK, Daddy?" Sasha asked.

"Oh, yes, my sweet" was his response. "Just allergies, I guess." He folded the map, and they drove slowly through town. The streets, scattered and desolate, dampened everyone's mood. A dog howled in the distance.

"We should find that dog and keep him!" Sasha chimed.

Marc glanced at Trudy and laughed. "I don't think so. He belongs to someone here."

Sasha pondered this for a moment and replied, "There are no people here! Are they all dead or in jail?"

Fortunately for Marc, he didn't have to think of an answer. A mile out of town, they came upon a farm. Two soldiers argued vehemently with a rough-looking woman, apparently the landowner. She refused to allow them past her gate.

Marc stopped and assessed the situation. "Trudy," he began, "I can take out these two rummies. Just keep my daughter's attention distracted, OK?"

Trudy started to gesture, but Jackie interrupted, "Hey, man, will the violence ever end?"

He turned to her and responded, "I really don't know. I'm not Sylvia the psychic!" Marc checked his gun, put on his jacket, and left the car to confront the three.

The argument centered on the woman's not having a stamped ID to sell eggs and other produce from the farm. Marc made a mental note of how this woman strongly favored the late great Janis Joplin. He hummed a few bars of "Me and Bobby McGee" as he approached. The two soldiers seemed annoyed. Marc kept his stride loose, casual. The soldiers, one approximately his own age, the other, probably Dylan's age, immediately stopped arguing and focused their attention on him.

The younger one snapped rather arrogantly at him. "What do you want, old man?" With a rapid single move, Marc spun the youngster around, grabbed his service pistol from his gun belt, and held it tightly against the soldier's right temple. "OK, kid, slowly, and I do mean, slowly, undo your gun belt and let it drop to the ground. Then your pants. I want to be sure you don't have an ankle piece!" He gestured to the older soldier and commanded, "You do the same, Sarge! Or I'll be forced to scatter your fucking brains all over this lady's farm! I'm sure it won't help her crop yield any!" Grudgingly the two obliged. The farmer chuckled. "Gather their weapons—they are now yours!" She collected their guns and tossed them in back of her truck. "Take their pants, lady. We're going to send the commandant a special message."

The older soldier handed the farmer both pairs of pants. Turning to Marc, he sneered, "You won't get away with this shit, asshole! We know who you are. There's a reward on your sorry ass, Mr. Former Ambassador! It's $50,000.00 if you're brought in alive!" Marc paused to contemplate this and nonchalantly responded, "Well, Sarge, this isn't your lucky day." He then promptly shot the officer in his head. The younger soldier urinated in his boxers. "Not such a badass now, are you?" Marc chided, still holding the gun against the youngster's temple. "This old man just took your gun, you lost your pants, and you just pissed yourself! I'd say that this is *not* your lucky day." The soldier refused to talk, so Marc marched him to the front gate, and the farmer tied his hands to a fence post. "Just like getting ready to castrate a hog!" She laughed demonically. Marc slapped a piece of duct tape across the solder's mouth. "No sense giving him a chance to yell for help." The soldier continued to urinate and struggled to free himself. The farmer held a pistol to his cheek.

Marc turned to see how his passengers fared. Trudy stared vacantly, her face void of any emotion. Anger flashed prominently across Jackie's attractive face. He surmised that Sasha hadn't seen any of this.

The farmer's gravelly voice broke the silence. "Are you really a wanted man? Damn!" she raged, "I don't need any more trouble!"

Marc smiled, gazing into her eyes. He helped her drag the dead soldier across the road and rolled his corpse into a drainage ditch. As they returned to the stench of the young soldier, Marc said, "Young lady, has anyone ever mentioned that you bear a strong resemblance to the late great rock star Janis Joplin?"

She stopped suddenly and barked, "Folks used to call me the Pig Lady. But now there ain't many folks around these parts no more! Tell your people that I want to talk to them now."

MEET THE PIG LADY

Marc motioned to the ladies seated in the car to come meet the Pig Lady. Sasha bounced right up to her and asked innocently, "Do people really call you the Pig Lady? Why?"

The Pig Lady answered, "Yes, child, they do. I raise pigs on this farm, and I also planted corn and other vegetables this year." Satisfied with her response, Sasha ran over to play with the chickens.

Trudy and Jackie introduced themselves. Pig Lady stated tersely, "Like I told your old man, I don't want no trouble. Looks like I got it, though."

Trudy quickly interjected, "He's not my husband. I am a widow."

Pig Lady nodded. "Yeah, I know. Just testing you." She pointed a gnarled finger at Marc. "I listened to a lot of shit about you and Dylan on TV. The government assholes really want you both!"

Marc agreed. "I'm not surprised. Dylan and the boys want to keep the fight going, while I'm trying to get us to my cousin Joel's gated community."

Pig Lady grinned and replied, "Well, by the looks of things, you can handle a gun, Mr. Ambassador!" Stunned, Marc started to respond, but Pig Lady dismissed him with a wave. "Hey, stud, I do watch TV after my chores. It was on the news when the embassy in whatever camel-shit country you were the ambassador to! I just never understand how you could work for an idiot of a president we had then! You damned near got your ass shot off over there!" Marc couldn't fault her logic.

"I understand what you're saying," he replied. "I just got caught up in all the drama and such."

Pig Lady appeared satisfied with that and reminded them, "You can't hang out here on my farm for long. It's only a matter of time before somebody comes looking for those soldiers. No one wants to fuck with me!"

Trudy flinched, offended by such coarse language. Marc tried to hide a grin. Jackie led Sasha to the car. Trudy followed without a word. Marc thanked Pig Lady for her hospitality, and the group resumed their journey. "How can you be so tolerant of such a buffoon?" Trudy raged. Jackie tried to intervene, but Trudy would have none of it.

"It never ends with you!" Trudy ranted. "You seem to thrive around crude and vulgar people!" Jackie made a halfhearted attempt to cover Sasha's ears.

Marc dodged a huge pothole in the road and replied, "You are just way too uptight about things. Your rosy-colored ideal world no longer exists! What the hell does it take to get through to you?" Trudy fumed in silence.

Moments later, they arrived in a small town. Fortunately, it offered a self-serve gas station. Marc stopped and filled up the car. Everyone got out to stretch. "Don't go into the station alone, everybody stay close!" Marc advised. "It's too quiet here!"

Trudy glared at him. Marc ignored her, opting to watch as Jackie and Sasha headed into the station to use the restroom. Still uneasy, Marc finished and went to pay. The cashier, an elderly gentleman, greeted him. "We don't get many civilians through here."

Jackie and Sasha used the restroom and stopped at a candy rack. Marc paid for the gas and simply replied, "Yeah, I'm surprised that the gas isn't being rationed."

The cashier laughed and stated, "Oh, it's supposed to be!"

Marc stared questioningly. The cashier continued, "I know how to alter records. You are a celebrity of sorts." Trudy entered the gas station at this moment. "The commandant wants you, Dylan, and the rest of your entourage badly. I'm not going to help them!"

Horrified, Trudy tried to speak. Marc slowly raised his hand and directed, "I think we need to go, *now*. Trudy, I think you finally get it." He thanked the cashier, and the four hurried to the Firebird.

Steve's clearly stressed voice erupted from the two-way radio, which was buried among Sasha's toys. "Can you guys hear me?" he cried. "We were outnumbered by soldiers when we tried to leave the state! So we came back and are holed up at Pig Lady's farm!" Jackie found the radio and handed it to Marc. Steve added excitedly, "There are two government sedans at the end of Pig Lady's driveway. They're questioning a half-naked soldier tied to a fence post!" Marc laughed and replied, "Hold your position. If necessary, shoot the bastards, all of them! We're coming back. Duke gave me a bag of grenades for emergencies. See you in a few minutes." Trudy's face paled.

Within five minutes, they reached the outskirts of Pig Lady's farm. Marc pulled off onto a service road. After retrieving the grenades from the trunk, he handed his car keys to Jackie and stated solemnly, "If I don't make it back, get yourselves to Cousin Joel's, you hear? You got a map, and so does your brother. There may be more soldiers showing up." Jackie scrambled into the driver's seat; Marc sneaked closer to the Pig Lady's driveway.

He slid behind some wild flowers adjacent to a junked vehicle and reached for the grenades. Oh, how lucky he felt to have been trained in so many areas of warfare by that disgruntled marine at the embassy. Without hesitation, he pulled the pins on two grenades, hurled them at the soldiers' sedans, and smiled at the resulting carnage. Jackie drove, parked a safe distance away, and watched the two sedans burn. Marc picked up the bag of grenades and joined the ladies. Sasha asked, "Are you having fun playing war, Daddy?" Trudy mumbled somewhat sarcastically. Jackie remained speechless.

Marc walked to Sasha, picked her up, and continued to watch the blaze. He hugged her, answering, "Yeah, it does look like a game, but it's not. There are bad people who don't want us to go to Cousin Joel's. So I have to stop them from hurting us."

Sam, Steve, and Dylan drove up and parked behind the Firebird. Dylan remained in the truck, while Steve and Sam joined the others. "Real smooth," Sam began. "You're as subtle as an elephant! Really, were those grenades necessary?"

Marc shrugged and replied, "Does it matter?"

Steve stepped between the two. "I radioed for them to come back! We're about out of ammo! I think we should just go straight to Joel's!"

Dylan and Sam were furious. "We agreed to keep fighting!"

Pig Lady intervened. "You guys aren't going to wage a war from here! You've already fucked up my operation just by being here!"

Marc turned and walked back to his car. Jackie looked after Sasha; Trudy raised her hands in despair. "When is this nightmare ever going to end?" She stormed off to the car.

Pig Lady continued to bitch at the guys after Marc and the women left her farm. "Just look at this damned mess! I'm sure there'll be more fucking soldiers following up on all the crazy shit that's happened here!"

Sam argued, "Wow! The thanks we get for helping you secure your farm! We're out of here!"

Dylan intervened, "No more arguing, *please*! Let's just go!" Pig Lady glared menacingly as the three left her farm.

Moments later, the tanks rolled across the farm. Pig Lady watched horrifically as one shot leveled the barn; a second shot scattered pigs from the sty. Soldiers fired rounds into her farmette, while the commanding officer collared her and cursed her in Russian. Pig Lady spit on him and, as a result, received a single bullet in her skull. The soldiers did not look back as they left the farm. The flames evenly spread throughout the once profitable farmland. Smoke billowed high into the sky. In town, the gas station attendant stepped outside momentarily to gaze at the black smoke.

The attendant returned to his customary place behind the counter when he noticed Sam and the guys drive onto the lot. Sam filled his gas tank, while Steve and Dylan went inside to purchase snacks. The attendant motioned them to watch his small portable television set.

THE EQUINOX NIGHTMARE

A government broadcaster interrupted the state newscast—live camera feed from Pig Lady's farm! Dylan and Steve stared, speechless with horror. Sam joined them as the cameras panned to all the dead soldiers. The newscast concluded with college photos of the three, with a phone number to call as well as a promise of a cash reward. Sam paid for the gas. The attendant stated in a level tone, "You guys better keep moving. The troops aren't far behind, and I'm a dead man for helping you!"

Dylan replied, "Even if we were captured, we'd never rat you out!"

The attendant smiled. "I know. When the troops get here, my sales will be checked. I haven't rationed gas. Go now, quickly!"

Dylan argued, "We'll take you with us!"

The attendant smiled again, this time, more nervously. He raised his shirtsleeve to show them a microchip emblazoned near his shoulder. "I appreciate the sentiment, Dylan, but it'd lead the soldiers right to you. Now, please go!"

Marc kept glancing in his rearview mirror, hopeful that the guys would soon catch up. Trudy turned on the radio, listening to the current news of troop activity. Jackie watched Sasha nap. When they reached a crossroad, Marc asked Jackie for the map. Trudy asked, "Are we lost?"

Marc answered quickly, "Oh, no, not at all. Just something doesn't seem kosher. A lot of open space, which bothers me. I like the seclusion of the wooded areas, especially those adjacent to farmlands." He studied the map for a few minutes then folded it and tucked it between his seat and the console. "Well, ladies," he concluded, "we might reach Joel's tonight without interruptions."

Trudy frowned as he resumed driving and questioned, "What do you mean by 'without interruptions'?"

Marc stated, "Oh, just no stops in small towns, no detours, no fights with troops."

Trudy cried, "Will the violence ever end with you?"

Marc patted the console and replied, "Still have a few grenades left to toss!"

She continued, "Why do I feel that it will never end with you?"

Marc pondered his response carefully. "There's a lot of wide open area, as you can see, before we reach the next town. That will be, um, Baymont. We have very little ammo left with which to defend ourselves!"

Steve offered to drive; Sam welcomed the break. "We've all studied the map," Sam reminded them. "Step it up a bit so we can catch the others. I'm not comfortable with my mom and my sister traveling with the ambassador of death!"

Dylan winced and offered, "He really was a decent teacher, and the loss of freedom has simply stressed him out."

Agitated, Sam argued, "Oh, is that it, stressed out? We weren't pinned down by those clowns in the sedans, and Marc comes to our rescue by tossing grenades? He's as nuts as his friend Duke!"

Steve gave his two pennies' worth. "Well, if he is nuts, do we want to join him at his cousin Joel's?"

Dylan ended the discussion, stating adamantly, "I'll take my chances. I need some rest, as well as a bit of time to regroup."

A light rain fell as the Firebird came into view.

The light rain became a steady drizzle as they neared Baymont. Sasha woke from her nap, whining to use the bathroom. "Hold on, we'll be in town in about three minutes," Marc encouraged and sped on into Baymont. Steve did the same. Dylan and Sam were somewhat nervous concerning the road conditions. Steve enjoyed speeding.

Marc felt relieved that small towns such as Baymont offered at least one convenience store. He drove into the Baymont Quick Mart and parked close to the entrance. Jackie carried Sasha inside, followed by Trudy and Marc.

While the ladies used the restroom, Marc grabbed a cart and chose some snacks and juice boxes for Sasha. He poured a cup of coffee for himself and wheeled the cart to the register. The clerk, a rather stuffy middle-aged woman, stated curtly, "I need to see your purchase identification."

Marc stared incredulously at her and pointed his gun in her face. "Ring up my purchases now or else I'll scatter your fucking brains all over those damned cigarettes, got it?"

The women exited the restroom with Sasha; Trudy screamed at the confrontation. Steve, Sam, and Dylan raced into the store. Sam shouted, "Have you lost your fucking mind, Marc?"

Marc kept the gun pointed on the cashier and, in a cold, level tone, directed Sam, "Lift up her shirtsleeves—there should be a microchip on one of her upper arms, out of plain sight." Sam refused to touch her. Dylan's curiosity got the better of him; he slowly lifted her sleeves. A microchip prominently implanted in her left arm unnerved him.

"I knew this would happen one day," Dylan said edgily.

The clerk refused to accept Marc's money and, from behind the counter, pressed a button. Everyone except Marc headed for the front doors. The doors would not open. "Oh, real cute!" Marc sneered. "She thinks she can hold us here for the troops! Think again, *bitch*!" With that, he shot out the glass in the doors, dumped the grocery cart, and followed the others out to their respective vehicles. No one spoke as they drove away.

A dense fog rolled in. *Marvelous,* Marc thought. He tried to text Cousin Joel and swerved onto the shoulder of the road, spraying gravel. Trudy ripped on him, "Pay attention to the damned road, will you *please?*"

Marc sent the text message. The reception was bad tonight. Marc ignored her and asked Jackie, "Hey, radio your brother and ask if they enjoyed our show at the Quick Mart." Jackie wasn't sure if he was serious.

Sasha chirped happily, "I had fun, Daddy! Are you a real cowboy?"

Visibility worsened as the fog grew more dense. Apparently, Joel hadn't received the text message. "We might be better off if we find a place to crash for the night," Marc advised. Jackie radioed the guys as they came upon a rather rustic motel.

Everyone gathered outside the motel office. "It makes me think of a horror flick I saw at a drive-in the summer I graduated high school—"

"Don't say it, this is your child here!"

Marc enjoyed this immensely, adding, "A true classic—*Motel Hell!*"

Dylan muttered, "One would probably have to be intoxicated to sit through it, assuming his date wasn't putting out!"

Trudy was outraged. Steve played peacemaker. "We are all exhausted. Let's just register in the office and get our rooms, OK?"

Sam stood quietly, watching the rain. He wondered aloud, "Is this a good idea? I know we need rest, but we're making ourselves easy targets! We don't have much ammo." The neon Vacancy sign crackled. Marc elected not to debate the issue any further. "I think we can have our choice of rooms," he said as he turned to enter the motel office. Everyone followed, glad to get out of the chilly night air.

The manager, an attractive fortyish woman, smiled warmly as she greeted them. "Good evening! I'm Marybeth. So good to have visitors! I don't have many these days, with restrictions on travel. Before that, the large motel chains—oh, well, enough of my business woes. Will you need two or three rooms?"

Dylan stepped aside as Trudy corralled her offspring. Steve slipped in behind Jackie. Trudy reached for the register and said, "Yes, my son, my daughter, her fiancé, and I will share one of your largest rooms."

Marybeth's smile disappeared rapidly, accepted the cash, and handed her a key to room 10. "It's quite spacious, ma'am. I'm confident that you all will be comfortable. The phones are operable. Call if there's anything you need."

Marybeth watched as Marc signed the registration for Dylan, Sasha, and himself. She waited till the others left for their room and spoke gently, "Your daughter is adorable. But you, Dylan, don't appear to be related."

Before Dylan could reply, Marc said, "We used to teach school, before it all changed."

Marybeth nodded understandingly and handed him the key to room 1. "It's still early. After you settle in, come back here. I'll put on a fresh pot of coffee. Marc, you bear a strong resemblance to my late husband."

Marc gestured to Sasha, who had begun to yawn. Dylan offered, "I'll get her settled in. You two should talk. Like she said, not many visitors here."

Marybeth offered Marc a handshake, which he readily accepted. "I'll be back soon," Marc stated. Sasha let Dylan pick her up and carry her, while Marc gathered needed items from the Firebird.

The room was clean, well furnished with two queen-size beds. Dylan laid Sasha down on one, and she promptly fell asleep. "Marc, I'm not going to sleep. You take the other bed."

Marc looked at him inquisitively. "Are you sure? We both need to rest. Hey, man, I don't plan to be visiting all night with our hostess, Marybeth. She does intrigue me, however." He grabbed his duffel bag and disappeared into the bathroom, returning fifteen minutes later comfortably attired in clean blue jeans, T-shirt, and sneakers.

Dylan razzed him. "You could at least shave—look like a real school teacher!"

Marc chuckled. "I'm only going to see her tonight!"

The rain lessened tremendously, but the fog persisted as Marc made the quick walk to Marybeth's office. She opened the door and scolded him, "You should wear a jacket!"

He just laughed and replied, "I'm inside now, it wasn't far!"

Marybeth invited him back to her lounge. "I made fresh coffee, baked some chocolate chip cookies today, and poured us a glass of milk. A light snack will help you sleep."

Steve watched through the venetian blinds of room 10. "You have got to see this," he called. "Marc is hooking up with the motel manager!" Sam and Jackie joined him, staring in disbelief. Trudy ignored them.

Sam wondered aloud, "Has he lost his mind?"

Trudy addressed her son. "You didn't have to listen to his crap all day today! I think he enjoys killing! Please be quiet, I need some sleep. I'll ride with you all tomorrow. Dylan can put up with Marc's nonsense!" Jackie and Trudy took the beds, Steve curled up on the sofa, and Sam repositioned a recliner to face the door in case there was a need to defend against intruders. "One cannot relax too much, even in this fog!"

Marybeth had already built a roaring fire in the fireplace and invited Marc to sit next to her on the sofa. He complimented her on her baking talents. She smiled warmly as he drank the entire glass of milk and asked, "What subject did you teach?"

He replied casually, "United States history since World War II and American government. Managed to annoy the board with complaints leveled against me for extensive intense discussion of the Kennedy assassination. I don't want to bore you with it, though."

Marybeth ran her hand on his thigh. "I can't imagine anything about you being boring!"

Marc caressed her hair.

Dylan settled in front of the window, watching the rain lessen and the fog intensify. Sasha slept soundly. He hoped Marc wouldn't stay out too late; he wanted to leave when the fog dissipated. He turned on the television. Reception was poor, and it was actually a relief *not* to have to listen to the commandant spew propaganda.

Marc sipped some coffee and munched on a chocolate chip cookie. "Why are you pulling away?" Marybeth asked.

He replied, "It's eerie being told I resemble your deceased husband. I'd like to get to know you, but I'm not going to be around that long." Marybeth pouted. Marc stood, continuing, "Something bothers me about you. You had no issue with accepting cash for the rooms. Won't that cause problems for you, dealing with the government later on?"

She answered quickly but carefully. "Even with martial law, not every business is under the commandant's control. Not yet anyway. I inherited this motel from my marital estate."

Marc rubbed his temples, feeling exhausted all of a sudden.

Concerned, Marybeth offered to get him some aspirin, of which he politely declined. She wrapped a plate of cookies for him to take to Sasha and Dylan and kissed him lightly on the cheek as he prepared to go. "I would have loved to hear your theories on JFK's assassination," she whispered in his ear.

He looked back at her briefly as he left her lounge and stated as he passed on through her office, "LBJ ordered the hit."

Dylan heard Marc walking up to their door and opened it to greet him. Marc handed him the plate of cookies and checked on

Sasha. Dylan settled back in front of the window and remarked, "You smell strongly of Marybeth's perfume. Did you have fun?"

Marc took off his shoes and socks, relaxing on the second bed. "No," he replied, "it's not what you think."

Dylan joked, "What did you do, share your views of Kennedy's murder with her?"

Marc drifted off to sleep and mumbled, "Yeah, something like that."

Dylan laughed and resumed watching the fog.

Marybeth stoked the dying embers in her fireplace, smiling slyly. Marc's propensity for talking in his sleep kept Dylan awake. Much of it was mere rambling, but several snippets motivated Dylan to turn off the television in order to hear clearly. The room had become very warm, and he searched for a thermostat. When he located it, the reading of seventy-two did not seem right.

"It's rather eerie, Dylan," Marc rasped heavily, "how I supposedly remind her of her dead husband. I do find her most attractive, but something's off. I'm not sure I want to know what it is." He turned over onto his stomach and slept soundly. Dylan pondered Marc's statements as he opened a window. He returned to his recliner and stared at the fog. *What a night,* he decided. *Should have asked him about* Motel Hell*!*

The remainder of the night passed uneventfully. Dylan helped himself to the cookies. Too bad there wasn't any milk. Sleep never came easy for him the longer he'd been on the lam. It was also becoming nearly impossible to do live remotes, to attack the commandant.

Marc awoke in a cold sweat. He tumbled out of his bed to check on his daughter, only to find her missing! He bolted to the door, furiously opened it, and saw her walking with Dylan to the motel's diner across the parking lot. The morning sun cut through some of the fog, improving visibility somewhat. The pleasant aroma of frying bacon tantalized his appetite. He closed the door and plopped back on the bed.

He felt as though he could sleep for several more hours. Dylan was apparently of the same opinion, having taken Sasha to breakfast. The room began to spin as he settled back on the pillows. Marybeth appeared at the foot of the bed, angry but silent. The strong essence of her perfume combined with hot, steamy vapors swirling about her caused Marc to squirm anxiously against the headboard, rubbing his eyes in disbelief. "No way," he stammered. "You, this is so wrong! You were very real, *alive*, last night! Is this some kind of fucking mind game you play with every guy who stops at this B-grade hole?"

Marc continued to rave. "You said I reminded you of your dead husband! What the fuck did you do, whack him over the head with a pan and bury his ass out back?"

Marybeth's eyes narrowed a fiery red, her hyena-like howl disturbing enough to unnerve even the most confident man. "You bastard! You just don't get it!" She hurled a table lamp at him. He rolled out of bed to avoid being struck.

"I get it that you're a real psycho, bitch!" he retorted and heaved a glass ashtray at her face. It sailed through the mist and shattered against the television. "Let me guess," he continued, "the commandant sent your nappy ass!"

Marybeth's image began to fade as she vowed, "You and Dylan will be captured then paraded through the town square like the lowlife thugs that you are!" Marc offered a one-finger salute in assessment of her final words. He scrambled unsteadily to his feet then collapsed heavily onto the bed. He tried to rise but felt paralyzed. Dylan and the others needed to be warned of Marybeth's intentions.

The open windows provided the room with a strong, fresh breeze. Marc slowly awoke, oblivious to his surroundings. He stared at the shattered television screen. *Damn, what a nightmare,* he thought. *Maybe I should have spent the night with her. Probably wouldn't have had the nightmare along with a damaged television to pay for.* He reached for his shoes and socks.

Once outside, he zipped up his jacket. Autumn had definitely arrived. He glanced in all directions before checking his weapon. *We must get to Joel's today,* he surmised. Only one clip left. He had no idea how much ammo Sam and Steve had. After securing his overnight bag in the trunk of the Firebird, he proceeded to the motel office. Marybeth must be at the diner, he assumed, when he entered and found it vacant. He hoped to pay for the damage in his room.

THE EQUINOX NIGHTMARE

Noticing some stationery with the motel logo near the register, he wrote her a brief note and attached some cash to it.

Marybeth joked loudly when Marc joined the others for breakfast. "Everyone wondered if you'd stay in bed all morning!" Marc looked at her, hoping to find some sign of ulterior motives but found none. Hell, he had been plagued with bizarre nightmares since he was Sasha's age.

He joined Dylan and Sasha in a booth and rubbed his eyes. Marybeth poured from a fresh pot of coffee. Marc thanked her and sipped slowly. "This is better than the Maxwell House I drank at home or in the teacher's lounge!"

Beaming, Marybeth said, "It is my own secret freshly ground brew! During better times, this diner was packed, and everyone said it was the coffee. Now, what would you like for breakfast?"

Marc replied, "No, thanks for asking, but my stomach's kind of feeble this morning. I didn't sleep too soundly last night. Must be the changing of the seasons."

Marybeth teased, "Maybe you ate too many cookies last night!"

Sam and Steve turned and stared.

Marc started to deny that and looked out the window. A convoy of military vehicles passed by. Marc squirmed nervously but said nothing. Marybeth returned to the kitchen. "We need to hit the road sooner rather than later," he whispered to Dylan.

Sam noticed the two former politicos huddled in conference form and joined them. "What are you two geniuses plotting?" he asked.

"Nothing yet," Marc replied as he looked out the window again to find a soldier snooping around his Firebird then on to check out Sam's truck. "I don't like this," he snarled. "Sasha, you stay with Dylan. Come to the car when you see me wave." He drew his gun and sped into the kitchen. Marybeth had gone, which instantly aroused his suspicions. He bolted out the back door and crept along the side of the diner, hoping to get a clear shot at the soldier, who now spoke in a Russian dialect on his radio. *Fuck this shit,* Marc decided as he drew his gun and aimed at the soldier's head. *Hopefully, my daughter isn't watching,* and he gently pulled the trigger.

WHERE DO WE GO FROM HERE?

Marc's confident smile as his single shot abruptly ended the soldier's existence faded instantly. Excruciating pain on the back of his skull led to unconsciousness. The pain still persisted as he wavered into semiconsciousness. Sasha and her new friend, a black girl approximately her age, stood over him with frightened expressions. Gunfire erupted nearby. An elderly woman shuffled to the sofa upon which he rested and introduced herself. Dylan joined her, poised to apply an ice pack.

"I'm Granny," she began. "This here's my grandbaby, Jasmine. You're safe here now." Turning to Dylan, she added, "You two been on TV all afternoon. Those government soldiers want you *bad*!" Marc struggled to sit up, but the pain returned. Dylan handed him the ice pack, while Granny admonished, "You be still now, you hear? You're in no shape to fight, let alone travel!" Dylan nodded in agreement. He moved quietly to the living room window, parted a curtain cautiously, and stated, "A soldier's checking the Firebird."

Sasha and Jasmine looked at Marc then gazed inquisitively at Granny. "Go to Jasmine's room now." The soldier continued to examine Marc's car. Dylan muttered, "I locked it, so you'll have to break a window to get in, you stupid ass!" Granny frowned.

Dylan continued to observe the soldier snooping around Marc's car. "You best take it easy, man. That's a hell of a bump on the back of your head!" Marc stared at him. Dylan related, "Our ol'-buddy Sam decided he didn't want Steve, Jackie, and Trudy to come with us to your cousin Joel's, so he smacked you with a wrench. That woman you were with at the motel ratted us out to the soldiers. I barely got you into the car. We made it into this town before running out of gas." He paused to permit Marc to absorb everything. "Sam's mom thought you were a bit psychotic. I tried to tell her we at times must defend ourselves. I have no idea where they went!" Marc nodded silently and settled back on the sofa. Dylan muttered an obscenity; the soldier radioed another officer, presumably.

Dylan moved away from the window and stated quietly, "It's a matter of time before this apartment complex is crawling with soldiers. We need to find another vehicle."

Granny responded, "Just us old folks is all that lives here. Soldiers never talk to us. We're no threat to them."

Dylan countered, "There's a first time for everything!"

As dusk approached, several soldiers arrived to examine the Firebird. Dylan seemed apprehensive. Granny lit candles. "Keeps the light bill low," she whispered, "and we can watch the parking lot without being seen. The soldiers are so used to most of us old folks turning in early." Dylan nodded silently; Marc wavered in and out of consciousness, mumbling incoherently.

"He has a concussion, I'm sure of it," Dylan opined.

Granny asked, "How did it happen? The soldiers?"

Dylan shook his head sadly, replying, "No, I'm afraid not. One of our own group. A college student, Sam. Their personalities clashed often. He didn't like his mom and sister riding with Marc in that Firebird. A lot of issues."

Granny listened intently; Dylan continued, "We're only about an hour's drive, according to the map in Marc's car, from reaching his cousin Joel's estate. It's a gated community." Jasmine and Sasha joined them. Granny nodded in Dylan's direction. He knew to weigh his words carefully in front of the youngsters.

Granny advised, "You all plan on settling in here for the night. Your leader's in no shape to travel." Smiling knowingly, she added, "I just can't believe we've met real freedom fighters that have been on TV!" Dylan tried to speak, but Granny held her hand up. "I know what you're thinking, young man. I know the risks of hiding fugitives. I am an old lady who's lived a long life. I only ask you take my grandbaby with you. It's only a matter of time before those goons start going door-to-door to question all of us." Jasmine started to protest. Granny stated, "Hush, child. These are good men. You'll have a shot at a life at Cousin Joel's. At sunup, I am going to create a diversion. Now y'all get some sleep, you hear?"

The girls giggled for a few minutes before falling asleep. Granny checked to be certain they were asleep then returned to the living room to speak with Dylan. She peeked out the window. "It's too dark now, but I am sure the soldiers are zeroed in on that car. You won't be able to get to it."

Agitated, Dylan said, "Our supplies are in there, along with what few weapons we have!"

Granny brought a tray of tea and cookies, with the hope of helping Dylan to relax. As she set the tray on the battered coffee table, Marc stirred and struggled to a sitting position. Dylan stared emotionlessly as Granny scolded, "Marc, you are more contrary than the children! You need to rest!"

He rubbed his temples and replied, "That's OK, I just need some aspirin. I'll rest when we get to Cousin Joel's." Dylan poured tea for all three; Granny held up her hand, motioning for silence. Marc moved quietly to the window. An explosion rocked the parking lot. Granny tumbled onto Dylan's lap. Marc staggered back against the wall. He turned carefully to peer out the window.

The Firebird, engulfed in flames, illuminated the parking lot like the set of a classic Sylvester Stallone action movie. A man who'd apparently been standing too close now screamed as he ran in an attempt to escape a fiery demise. He soon collapsed onto the parking lot. Several soldiers gathered to watch as his screaming slowly waned.

Granny shook her head sadly. "That was Old Man Jeffries. He always took his trash out after dark. We all knew he liked to bury his booze bottles in the Dumpster!" Marc leaned into the wall, perspiring heavily. "We have to carry you piggyback. I will do it! You won't last five minutes against those God-forsaken storm troopers!"

Before she could protest, Dylan stood up, declaring, "He's right. We can't leave you here. Do you have a vehicle we can use?"

Sasha and Jasmine joined them. Granny stated, "Yes, just outside the back door, a white Buick. My husband bought it new in 1981. It still runs nice!"

Granny hurriedly dressed the girls and packed food and snacks into their book bags. Marc found the aspirin in the bathroom closet, took four tablets, and pocketed the bottle. Dylan moved furniture to barricade the front door. Anything to slow the soldiers, as they now pounded on neighbor's doors. Marc contemplated starting a small blaze on the pile of furniture barricaded against the door, but Dylan jingled the keys Granny had just given him. "Come on, man," he whispered, "we have to go now! It's time!" The back lot seemed almost too quiet, but all five managed to scramble into the Buick undetected. Dylan turned the key and started the engine. Marc looked back at Granny and the girls, nodding approvingly. This car ran so quietly compared to his Firebird. Dylan maneuvered carefully around other parked cars, relying only on parking lights.

As they neared the western edge of the lot, Granny directed, "Dylan, put your headlights on. There's an old service road. Take it, watch out for any loose gravel. Just go slow, no one ever goes this way anymore. It'll take us to the main highway." Dylan continued on. The girls fell asleep as Dylan turned north on State Highway 47. A half-moon emerged from the clouds. Granny and the girls slept soundly as they finished the journey to Cousin Joel's estate. Dylan and Marc were relieved the trip ended without any further incidents. A majestic sunrise illuminated the gated community in which Joel's estate centered. Dylan and Marc sat stoically as the main gate opened slightly, and a security officer approached.

Dylan made the introductions. The officer responded, "Yes, Joel is expecting you. He mentioned you'd be traveling in a classic Firebird, a 1971 model, I believe."

Marc turned to him and stated, "Yes, we had some adventure along the way, and it became necessary to change vehicles."

The officer radioed for a nurse. "For the girls and the grandmother. Joel believes a feminine presence helps the young people in transition. And, Marc, I'll need your gun."

Marc frowned and reluctantly turned over his weapon.

The nurse arrived momentarily. Dylan and Marc got out of the car and gently awakened the girls. The girls clung to Dylan. "We want Granny to come along too!" Sasha insisted.

Marc hugged his daughter and whispered, "Go with the nurse. We'll be along soon, OK?"

The nurse introduced herself. "I'm Karen. Your daddy and Dylan have a few grown-up things to do, and soon we'll all eat a nice breakfast with Joel!"

The security officer waited until the girls and Nurse Karen were well out of earshot before speaking. "I notice that the grandmother appears somewhat pallid."

Marc opened the door and attempted to nudge Granny. "Wake up, we've finally made it!" he urged.

Dylan reached in to check her pulse. Stunned, he staggered back and exclaimed, "She's dead!"

Marc, Dylan, and the officer stared, speechless. The officer also checked Granny and calmly confirmed Dylan's diagnosis. He radioed for another officer, who arrived immediately. "We will want to talk with you two in the main office. Please turn over the keys to the car. As you can readily see, we are very self-sufficient here. We do have a funeral parlor in this community. Dylan, please turn over the keys to this officer, and then you and Marc may enter our community. We will start the orientation process in the main security office." Dylan handed over the keys, and the officer drove Granny into the downtown area. The first officer invited Dylan and Marc in and closed and secured the gate. Without a word, the three men walked to the security office nearby. Marc observed the surroundings. Part of the downtown may have been hit early on in the occupation. Caution tape encircled the rubble of a minimall.

THE EQUINOX NIGHTMARE

Dylan and Marc were directed to be seated at desks in a classroom setting. Each then received an application. "We like to see how new people will adapt to our community," one officer stated as his partner drove the Buick to the funeral parlor. "Joel started the policy. We all have jobs to do here, everyone serves as purpose." He accepted a call at his desk. "Yes, yes," he stared at them. "I'll be right over. Yes, I will advise them of your policies. Especially because Marc is your cousin." He ended the call and stated, "I have another matter to attend to, and then I will return in a few minutes to escort you both to see Joel. Finish your apps, please." He turned and left the room.

They finished their applications and looked out the front window. "It sure seems odd," Marc began, "that no one is out on the streets. It is a nice, sunny day."

Dylan agreed, and replied, "True. Other than that mess at the minimall, it appears to be a well-maintained community. It's strange that no one is working to clean it up."

Marc nodded and continued, "I wonder who'll clean it up. I wonder if Sam, Steve, Jackie, and Trudy came here. Regardless of the issues they had with me, I hope they're safe, wherever they chose to go."

Approximately an hour passed, and no one returned to escort Dylan and Marc to see Cousin Joel. "Let's go explore this place," Marc stated. "My patience has run out! Besides, I'd like to know where they've taken the girls."

Dylan agreed, and they left the office. The sun shone brightly, seemingly to revitalize the men. Marc pointed at the shambles of the minimall, and they checked it out. Marc raised the caution tape, and they headed for the main entrance. Dylan offered, "I bet this area fell early, before Joel and his people were able to secure their community."

Surprised to find the doors unlocked, Marc replied, "I don't know. I haven't talked to Joel since we were in high school. We just didn't stay in touch. I really don't know what he did before our government collapsed. My wife, Ginny, handled all our Christmas cards and such while I was the ambassador."

They passed variety shops and a food court, all in need of repair. Marc noticed a new padlock on the mall security office door, tapped Dylan's shoulder, and gestured. Dylan frowned; he believed it to be rather odd. Just beyond the fountain, a roof had collapsed on a clothing store. Low moaning sounds emanated from the rubble. Thinking that some workers may have been injured, they hurried to the fountain. Dylan advised, "We best be careful climbing on this damn rubble. It might further collapse!" Marc nodded. The moans were barely audible now. Slowly and cautiously they scaled the rubble, and upon reaching the top, they gasped at the sight in the huge crater. The men stared, speechless. Mutant figures feasted on the corpses of Granny, Sam, Steve, Jackie, and Trudy! Dylan counted eight mutants; Marc remained silent. Finally, he mustered a horrific gasp. "What the fuck has Joel got going on here?" The mutants heard what he had said, and all eight slowly lumbered toward them. Marc took a half step back and almost tumbled backward into the fountain. Dylan searched frantically for anything that could be used as a weapon. Both stumbled slightly as they moved away from the oncoming mutants. "Steady wins this race, Dylan," Marc mumbled. "They don't move that well in this debris."

Dylan nodded and replied, "True. Let's lure them to that fountain, see how they deal with water."

Marc nodded, and as they passed the fountain, all eight tumbled downhill into it.

Dylan and Marc watched the mutants splash about in the fountain. "It'll take a bit for them to climb out," Marc stated. "Let's see if we can slow a couple of them down, maybe kill them." Dylan grabbed two pieces of wood, splintered from the roof's collapse. He handed one to Marc, who hurled it like a spear. The pointed end shattered mutant Sam's skull at its cerebral cortex. Mutant Sam dropped in a mess of bone, decayed skin, and congealed liquid of some sort on a fountain step.

"I knew you'd do that," Dylan said as he fired his splintered wood at mutant Steve, decapitating it. Mutant Steve's skull floated like a child's beach ball in the fountain. Joel watched this with great amusement on close-circuited television in his office. "Your cousin

THE EQUINOX NIGHTMARE

can fight," commented Joel's security director. Joel nodded and turned to glance as Marc's ex-wife, Ginny, strolled amiably to Joel's desk. Joel patted her slender backside; Ginny beamed seductively.

Joel answered, "We will see what he and Dylan are capable of." He sent a text message.

Ginny inquired, "What do you have in mind?"

Joel boasted, "I just directed Mikey to unleash more mutants into the minimall. Ginny, my dear, please go get Sasha and her friend Jasmine from the nurse's station."

Dylan and Marc continued their exploration of the devastated minimall. "I'd guess that Cousin Joel has some misguided and devious activity in progress," Marc summarized.

Dylan agreed and asked, "What do you suppose he's trying to accomplish? This is as sick and unethical as the shit pulled in the Nazi death camps over seventy years ago!"

Joel pulled Ginny onto his lap and continued to view the TV screen. Ginny warned, "Do not underestimate him, Joel. He is very analytical. Persistent bastard as well. Never thought he'd even make it here!" She kissed Joel and started for the nurse's station.

Sasha and Jasmine soon grew restless, having read all the children's books in the nurse's office waiting room. The girls sauntered over to the window, watching curiously as Dylan and Marc walked into the minimall. As they turned to leave, Ginny entered and exclaimed, "How is my baby girl? Oh, and you have a new friend! How nice!"

Sasha sneered, "Yeah, and it was real nice how you left me and Daddy!"

Ginny knelt to hug her daughter, but she scurried out the door, followed by Jasmine. Ginny phoned Joel's desk, informing him of what had just occurred. "Our security officers will find them.," Joel replied.

Sasha and Jasmine hid behind Dumpsters as Joel's officers passed by. The two friends eyed Danger and Do Not Enter signs at a side entrance of the minimall. "Come on," Sasha urged, "we got to find my daddy and Dylan. This is a bad place!"

As they scurried through the broken door, Jasmine asked, "Was that lady really your mama?"

Sasha replied, "Who cares? She left me, my Daddy, and my nanny, Adrienne."

Ginny returned to Joel's office, and a heated exchange ensued. Joel attempted to calm the fiery redhead, but Ginny insisted on giving him her two pennies' worth. "You lying bastard! You said they'd never find out what the fuck we're doing here! If those two brats find Marc and Dylan, it's all over for us, our life's work!"

Joel blasted, "Shut the fuck up! You're not exactly Mother of the Year, you crazy bitch! You're the one who left your husband and kid to be with me and develop these killer soldiers! Relax, the mutants Mikey turned loose should separate our wannabe heroes from the girls. He just finished cremating Granny. She was old, and her body parts could not benefit our work."

Ginny fumed but said no more. She poured a glass of scotch. Joel smiled arrogantly and read from his notes. "We've done well in terms of altering their genetics upon reviving them. Still, we have to find ways to improve their physical coordination."

Ginny poured a second drink and sipped thoughtfully before she responded, "In time, I believe we can fix that, but for the time being, I think we should be glad that when our undead soldiers bite a living human prisoner, the prisoner *turns* into one of them!"

Joel shuffled some papers then looked directly at her. "I agree, but at some point, we will need more space not only to contain them but to work on correcting the issues of coordination. Some of those injections we used early on may have permanently destroyed the bone structure."

Ginny seemed to calm herself, finished her drink, and said, "But we never banked on Marc and his friends getting past the soldiers at Duke's farm! You really should never have invited him here. I tell you, he is worse than that old NBC-TV detective Columbo!"

Joel smiled and poured some scotch. "I have no doubts about his talents," he began, "but cannot believe that he and Dylan will get past all those mutants! The looks of them, they are barely able to function."

Ginny shook her head. "No. Don't underestimate him. He's not afraid of a fight. Those marines in the embassy taught him a lot!"

Dylan and Marc examined the entrance of a sporting goods store. "There may be weapons!" Dylan happily declared.

Marc cautioned, "We have to watch out. I'm not sure that Joel hasn't created a lot more of those things! I'm hungry. Hopefully they have protein bars or some kind of snack food."

Dylan nodded, and they slowly entered.Sasha and Jasmine waited till the soldiers passed then sneaked through a service entrance door. Soon they found they'd happened upon a food court. Sasha turned on a light. Jasmine worried aloud, "Are you sure we should have a light on? I mean, those soldiers!" Her voice trailed off sadly.

Sasha answered, "Just long enough to find a fridge with some good food!"

Jasmine handed her a bag of corn chips.

Mikey reported back to Joel and Ginny. The two stopped arguing and stared at him. "I have turned about twenty of those things loose!" he stated proudly. "No way in hell they'll get out now!"

Joel was not so sure. "He and Dylan just went into a sporting goods store. Depends on what they find to fight with. We never did check what merchandise remained when we fenced in that shithole!"

Ginny watched the TV and screamed, "The girls are in the food court!"

Mikey muttered, "It's not like you gave a shit about the kid."

Joel raised his head, gestured at the screen.

Sasha and Jasmine ate and drank their fill, bagged some snacks as well as energy drinks before warily opening the food court door and peeking out on the mall. Sasha pointed at the food court door and peeked out on the mall. Sasha pointed at Marc and Dylan as they entered the sporting goods store. She called out "Daddy!" and both girls began running toward the store. Apparently, Marc and Dylan hadn't heard her call out. The girls stopped suddenly as mutants staggered out of the fountain. More limped out of a jewelry store, having been released by Mikey, Both girls slowly stepped back and hurled snacks and drinks at the mutants in the hope of slowing their progression. Sasha screamed again for her dad; both raced back to the food court and barricaded themselves in with tables and chairs.

Dylan and Marc helped themselves to pistols and ammo. Both heard Sasha's scream, and they ran out of the store. "There's too many of them!" Dylan shouted. "I can't see them!"

Angrily Marc bitched, "They may have run into a store. We got enough to shoot the entire herd of those fucks! I'll be sure to save one for my idiot cousin!"

Dylan nodded and replied, "For sure! Remember to aim at their heads!"

The two men proceeded to shoot the entire herd in a most methodical fashion. As the final mutant toppled into a decorative planter, Marc tucked his pistol in his jacket pocket and rubbed his temples gingerly. "You OK?" Dylan asked.

Nodding, he replied, "Yeah, just a migraine, is all. The noise of the gunfire doesn't help matters any."

Dylan surveyed the heap of dead mutants and stated, "We shouldn't try to climb over the mess. Even a slight scratch may infect us with whatever shit infected them!"

Marc agreed. "Yes, that is for sure. I am saddened to say that these were once human beings, loved ones with families and friends."

Dylan added, "Yes. We must say good-bye to Sam, Steve, Jackie, and Trudy."

Marc stated sadly, "Yes, and the one dangling from the fountain sure does look a lot like Sasha's nanny, Adrienne."

Their remembrances were soon interrupted by the screams of two frightened girls. "Help us, we are in the food court!" Sasha shouted.

Marc yelled, "There's too many of these damn things piled up, We can't get through where you came in! Do not make a sound till Dylan and I knock on the food court door and call out for you, understand?"

Silence followed.

Dylan whispered, "I believe they got it." They reloaded their weapons and made their way out as they had entered and, within minutes, reunited with Sasha and Jasmine. The four ducked behind a nearby Dumpster as two of Joel's security officers passed by driving Granny's Buick. Marc stared, fuming silently, his gun drawn. Joel and Ginny continued their argument after listening to the gunfire. "I tried to tell you, you dumb ass!" Ginny ranted. "Marc is very resourceful. I am certain that his friend Dylan is as well. Are you fucking trying to ruin all we have accomplished?"

Mikey entered and intervened on Joel's behalf. "No need to worry, Ma, I got security out looking for them. It's only a matter of time before we round them up!"

Ginny lashed back at her son. "You shut the fuck up! You were supposed to finish them off! Now all our work has been destroyed!"

Mikey, accustomed to his mother's rants, drank from Joel's bottle of scotch and belched crudely. Ginny glared at him. Joel sat back in his chair with a confident smirk, enjoying the tension that permeated the room. Finally, he spoke, truly savoring this moment. "There's no place for them to run—hell, we got this place locked down tighter than the commandant's ass!" Mikey swigged from the bottle of scotch and stared proudly at a portrait of the commandant that hung on the wall behind Joel's desk. Ginny started to reply, but Joel raised his right hand and continued, "They got two little girls slowing them down, no food or water, unless they found some in that food court, as much ammo as they can carry, and a total ignorance of the layout of our community!" Mikey finished off the scotch and radioed security for a status update. He received no answer.

On the second passing of Granny's car, Marc tossed a rock and bounced it off the trunk. The officers stopped and got out to search. Jasmine peeked out from behind the Dumpster and howled, "You stole my granny's car!" The officers ran to her, in hopes of capturing her, but Dylan and Marc emerged from a nearby shrubbery. Each bludgeoned the officers into unconsciousness with bricks in an effort to avoid noisy, attention-gathering gunfire.

THE END OF THE LINE

Without a word to Ginny and Joel, Mikey sped out of Joel's lair to personally check the status of his security officers. He radioed the officers once more and became angry at the lack of response. He turned to his right and apprehensively stared at the unmanned Buick now parked in the town's park. Electing not to radio Joel, he approached cautiously, his gun drawn.

Dylan and Marc observed Mikey with justifiable trepidation. "Do you think it was wise to make the girls hide behind the jungle gym?" Dylan whispered.

Marc nodded. "I hope so. It just seems to be the safest, most durable, in the event we have an exchange of gunfire." Mikey circled the unattended vehicle, stopped at the trunk, and stared intently as he comprehended the relevancy of blood smears on the trunk as well as the bumper.

Marc aimed his pistol at Mikey as he radioed Joel. "I'm not sure I want to open the trunk!" he whimpered. Marc squeezed the trigger at the same time Joel barked, "Do it, damn you!" They watched in horror on Joel's computer as fragments of Mikey's skull and brain matter splattered on the Buick. Ginny screamed and fainted. Joel slammed his laptop shut and cursed his cousin, realizing his world dominance scheme was soon to end. "Why did you have to kill that kid? I sure hope the girls didn't see it! Why?" Dylan demanded.

Marc stood and turned to his friend, emotionless. "It had to be done, old friend," he began. "That piece of work is my former stepson, Mikey. It means that my ex-wife, Ginny, is mixed up in this shit with my idiot cousin!" Dylan shook his head sadly.

Joel revived Ginny, who in turn promptly slapped him. "You bastard!" she seethed. "My son is fucking dead because of you! Our work is ruined too because of you, you pompous ass!" Joel tried to calm her, but she'd have none of it. She grabbed a paperweight and attempted to hit him with it, but he grabbed her wrist and bent it till she dropped it. "You know I can't let you live since obviously I can no longer trust you, bitch!" Joel stated calmly. She glared defiantly. With a surgeon-like precision, he strangled her, talking to her throughout his murderous act. "We had a good thing going. I only wanted you just to say I have my cousin's old lady! But the commandant liked what I had going on here, the genetic experiments and all. Now I'm going to have to kill Marc and the rest!" She struggled weakly as he applied a final twist, snapping her neck.

A frenzied thought process dominated Joel's already troubled mind. He picked up Ginny, carried her to the window, and heaved her lifeless body through it. Sasha and Jasmine emerged from behind the jungle gym, speechless. Pale in demeanor, they ran to Dylan and Marc, screaming hysterically.

Dylan stood first, having hidden behind an abandoned ice cream van. Joel's first shot nicked him on his earlobe; the second shot hit squarely in his chest. Marc emptied his pistol into Joel's already broken window, and three poorly aimed shots struck Ginny's corpse. The girls ran to the jungle gym and covered their ears, frightened over the shoot-out in progress. Marc scrambled to Dylan, oblivious of the shouts of the townspeople who had come out to survey the scene. Marc applied pressure to Dylan's wound, but Dylan began to choke up blood. "Hang in there, Dylan!" he pleaded frantically and screamed at the gathering throng, "What are you staring at, you fucking idiots? This man needs medical attention, *now*!" Everyone stood silently. Finally, a young woman burst through the crowd, first aid kit in hand.

Dylan spit more blood and stated weakly, "No, Marc. It's almost over for me. Save the girls, and *please*, just for me, take out that psycho cousin of yours! Do it, man!" He closed his eyes. The woman shook her head sadly.

Marc reloaded his pistol and ran to the building, realizing he must kill his cousin. Joel peeped out the window and knew he must make his escape. He began to pour bottles of hard liquor all over his desk. *No way in hell is he going to learn the nature of my work,* Joel decided and lit some old newspaper pages and tossed it on the liquor-saturated floor. Flames engulfed the buildings as Marc kicked in the door; the intensive heat drove him back onto the porch. Joel barely escaped the flames by staggering out the back door. He hoped to elude Marc or any other resident of the gated community by running north on Main Street. Several persons attending to Dylan, as well as one who raced to Marc's aid, noticed Joel on the lam. Blinded with rage, Marc pushed himself to his feet, refusing offers of assistance.

Sasha and Jasmine peered at the chaos from the jungle gym. Marc shouted, "Stay put, girls! Joel is a bad man!" Joel turned and ran into the minimall. Marc drew his gun and followed him. At the food court service entrance, Joel stopped suddenly and began shooting at Marc. Marc dove behind construction debris and returned fire. Once inside, Joel began setting fires and escaped out the north entrance, bounding over a fence into a forest preserve.

Residents worked tirelessly to extinguish the fires set by their former captor. Sasha and Jasmine joined Marc as he made his way back to Dylan. "Is he dead?" Jasmine asked. Marc nodded. Sasha started crying; Jasmine consoled her. Marc hugged both girls.

"What about my granny?" Jasmine ventured. Marc nodded once again.

The rains came as the residents brought the two fires under control. By Marc's quick count, at least twenty-five persons huddled together in the picnic shelter near the jungle gym. Several ladies organized a potluck supper and asked Marc to speak. The men who'd been tending to the fire joined them, the now torrential downpour aiding in their efforts. Marc thanked the ladies and stood, leaning on a picnic table to steady himself.

Everyone ate as he spoke, at his insistence. "I am sure we'll never know exactly what my cousin Joel did here," he began, "but now it is our responsibility as a free people to remain that way. I don't know what our future holds, but we must secure this community *soon*! Joel escaped, but he may reach the commandant. While we are rebuilding, we must have round-the-clock security. Anyone who is proficient with weapons may join this detail. Thank you."

As Marc sat to enjoy a plate of food offered him, the community's nurse observed the bump on the back of his head. Upon careful examination, she stated emphatically, "You, sir, will *not* be pulling guard duty anytime soon. I order you to rest!" Marc chuckled and introduced himself. She replied, "I'm Amanda. Your charm and wit will not make me change my mind." The rain slackened to a drizzle, and the men stopped by Marc's table for introductions. One offered to head up a resident's council, an idea Marc wholeheartedly supported. With that, Amanda declared, "OK, that will be enough. Marc will stay tonight in our infirmary. The girls can stay with me. It'll be sundown in less than an hour. Let's begin securing our community now." The men began to disperse; it was apparent everyone knew the importance of their roles.

Amanda took Marc's arm and led him to the infirmary. "What are you thinking, my new friend?" she asked.

Marc, suddenly feeling tired after the meal, sighed. "Oh, a multitude of thoughts. I hope this is the beginning of a decent life. Sasha and Jasmine need stability. We've been on the run for way too long."

Amanda nodded understandingly. "Yes, I see what you're saying. Your cousin strictly regulated our television-viewing habits. Only state-sponsored programs. More like propaganda."

By the time they reached the infirmary, the rain ceased completely, and a corpulent, fiery sun emerged from storm clouds in the west. A slight yet noticeable rainbow formed. "I believe that's a good sign." Amanda gazed ecstatically. Marc remained silent; the migraine had returned. She turned to him and inquired, "Are you feeling ill?" Marc brushed aside her concern. He simply wanted to watch the sunset.

The townspeople went on about their tasks. Marc and Amanda continued to watch the sunset, oblivious to the passersby. "This is beautiful," she leaned in to whisper. "We need to have a nice, peaceful name for our community."

Marc pondered her comments and responded, "Back home, the azaleas were sure lovely at this time of year. When we could, Ginny and I liked to sit on our porch, just looking at them and watching the summer sun set."

Amanda masked a gasp, knowing it would be unwise to tell him of the extent of Ginny's relationship with Joel. *We need him healthy,* she decided as they turned to go inside. He followed without a word. "What are you thinking, Marc?"

He simply responded, "Not much. I doubt that JFK envisioned this kind of America on that trip to Dallas long ago…"

ABOUT THE AUTHOR

Mark has been writing in a variety of genres since his first creative writing class at O'Fallon Township High School in southern Illinois, 1979. When he is not busy writing, Mark is a tireless advocate for the needs of those suffering from mental health issues to have cuts in their services restored to proper levels, after draconian cuts by three previous Illinois state governments' administrations. He has published articles regarding this serious health issue in a number of newspapers since 2009. Mark's other hobbies include watching the Chicago Cubs, studying U.S. History Since WW II, & entertaining friends as the area's only known Ringo Starr impersonator. Inspiration for "The Equinox Nightmare" came from a WW II veteran of the U.S. Army, Robert Pierpoint, who mentored Mark during his teenage years. Other WW II veterans who have influenced Mark include: Robert Batt, Lloyd Hoff, & Delbert Spitz. Thank you for your service, Sirs!